"A depth of experien[ce]
people share such dee[p]
a gift to be the recipie[nt]
and consciousness. Indeed we are profoundly reminded that we are One being experiencing ourselves as the many. A unique read for the open hearted."

~ Nina Zimbelman, Director, Gleanings Foundation

"An inspiring story given with love to awaken us to our purpose and life agreement from the perspective of the Native American, yet written in a way to unite us all."

~ Amber Suter, LMT, Holistic Healing Practitioner

"GY Brown and PH Jones have crafted a novel that is not only entertaining, but conveys a vital message about prophesy and spirit. From its captivating introduction, *7 Days to Forget* leads the reader on a spiritual journey through the essence of Lucas. By focusing on the microcosm of family, Brown and Jones' novel reminds us that we are all a part of the something bigger."

~ Catherine Rayburn-Trobaugh, freelance writer

"This is an engaging three-generational story of learned wisdom, love, and soul-connection from the perspective of Native American healers, informed by their prophecies and beliefs about the nature and purpose of the human experience. It gave me hope that our fractured, toxic, disintegrating civilization may be transformed into one of communion with each other and with this precious ball on which we live."

~ Katherine Lynch, M.D.

"*7 Days to Forget* offers timely universal wisdom through an engaging story colored with ancient Native American teachings. Everyone can benefit from the empowering message."

~ Terrie Jiang, educator

"Finally! A book that allows parents to relax and let their children be children. This book successfully ties our past with our present and our future while explaining that it is okay to remember and talk about all three. It reminds us that all of these are woven together, much like an intricate basket.

If you realize that your child is a 'good kind of different' and feel that he or she can't possibly fit into the square pegs of society, then you MUST read this book! Your perspective will forever be changed."

~ Phyllis Fuller, educator and mother

"As an interfaith minister, I am drawn to the mystical wisdom traditions of world faiths and even quantum physics as languages for holding the truth of our oneness. Sometimes these languages can seem very remote from daily life, so I can find myself alone traversing the ground between brain and heart. In *7 Days to Forget*, an ever-present character is Ms. Abby who acts as a loving guide, sharing the wisdom of the ancestors. As I read this book, I became aware of a magical connection between the stories on the pages and what was happening in 'real' time. I had my own Ms. Abby in GY Brown and PH Jones, who held my hand and whispered in my ears, connecting me deeply and directly to their sacred teachings.

I'm grateful to be able to encourage each of you to open your hearts to the knowing that arrives through this book, one story and character at a time. These words speak to the child inside you who has never forgotten the agreements you made, choosing your path to healing and service in this lifetime.

Prepare to remember."

~ Rev. Donna Belt, Interfaith Minister

7 Days to Forget

This book is dedicated to
the children of the future.

Inside Me Are the Spirits

Inside me are the spirits of those who were before,
And they will always walk with me no matter what's in store.
They smile with me, they laugh with me, they dry away my tears,
And I will never be alone, there's nothing I should fear.

We are the children of the future.
We are the children of the Earth.
And we are the people who can change the world
if we remember, if we remember....

The children who will follow will have my memory,
And they will feel me close to them wherever they might be.
They'll feel my touch and hear me as I whisper through the trees,
And they will never be alone, I'll be there in the breeze.

Music by PH Jones
Words by GY Brown and PH Jones

7 Days to Forget
Copyright © 2010 by GY Brown and PH Jones
Cover design by GY Brown

Inside Me Are the Spirits
Copyright © 2011 by PH Jones and GY Brown
Music by PH Jones
Lyrics by GY Brown and PH Jones

All rights reserved.

No part of this book may be reproduced in any form or by any electronic or mechanical means including information storage and retrieval systems, without permission in writing from the authors.

Sale of this book without a front cover may be unauthorized. If the book is coverless, it may have been reported to the publisher as "unsold or destroyed" and neither authors nor the publisher may have received payment for it.

7 Days to Forget is a work of literary fiction. Any resemblance to actual persons, both living and dead, events, or locations is entirely coincidental.

Printed in the United States of America

Visit us at **www.7daystoforget.com**

ISBN-13: 978-1463673376

ISBN-10: 146367337X

7 Days to Forget

GY Brown
PH Jones

PART I

Lucas

Chapter 1

I lay on my death bed, peering out beneath closed lids at my grieving family. I was amused that they acted as though this death business was a bad thing. It occurred to me that it looked like I was viewing them through pin holes in Dixie cups. The thought would have made me chuckle if I had been able.

The biggest surprise was that the people around me could not hear or understand what I was saying now any better than they could my first day on this planet. I had spent my life teaching communication, having taught thousands of students in my 30 years as a high school English teacher.

Yet now, at this critical time in my life when there was so much to say, not one of the people closest to me could understand a word or thought. It was ironic, really.

This was one of those times when humans openly seek comfort from the unseen and cry out for the truth. Truth, reality, and remembering grow strong in the fertile, broken ground of sorrow.

If only they would be silent, they would hear the thoughts and know.

The thought-words floated around with no place to land. It was as if my family's constant babble was scaring them away. The knowledge of the life agreement each had made when they came here was right in front of them. The deep desire of all humans to understand the agreement that keeps them here when life gets tough could be theirs in this moment. Comprehension of how our beings are fused with our Spirits was only a blink away.

Would you all please just listen?

Even as I shouted the words in my mind, I realized I was powerless to make them hear. The only thing that shouting did at this point was to make the smooth waves around me turn to jagged lines.

I realized sadly that they couldn't see either. The Spirits were all around us, and I recalled how Ms. Abby taught that we are never alone. We are always surrounded by Spirits, and we constantly interact with the rest of Creation. It was important to her, I remembered, that we respect the space we inhabit, realizing that we share both space and time simultaneously. It was critical in her teachings that we watch our step in theory and reality. I had not fully understood any of this until now.

How can you just keep bumping into the Spirits hovering around us? Be careful! That was your child – my grandson – you just ran though! He might not even want to come if you aren't more careful! All this crying and moaning is frightening. Who wants to spend a life in that?

Don't make your choice too quickly, dear grandson. It really is a good place for your life experience. They are usually more considerate of another's space, I promise. Please look at the whole picture. Grief is ruling their actions at this moment. They are in fear of the change that my crossing over means to them. They do not remember that death is not the end. They will really need you to help them understand the reality shift that will frighten them in the days to come.

My pleadings would have no impact on my grandson Jack's decision. I had no control over that. But the fact that I loved and respected my family could influence his decision. He could feel my love filling the room, surrounding those I loved the most as I prepared to cross over.

I found the opportunity to communicate with my grandson-to-be a spectacular and unexpected blessing. It had made me sad to think that I would cross before he was born and that I might never know him. The awe of the moment provided the comforting sensation of oneness. This oneness was deeply spiritual and profoundly eternal. I moved forward to communicate in the dialog of sameness, settling into the soothing comfort that all thoughts were known. There was no need for words in the oneness.

We both know, Jack, that these are the days of prophecy fulfillment. You know what you are coming to this place to do. You and others of your generation are gifted in seeing the unseen and hearing the unspoken. We see the children that are being born with the knowing. We sense that newborns can still see long after they agree to stay and can help those who have forgotten how to understand.

Many appear to be the reincarnation of those from other cultures with the knowing from centuries of awareness. Ms. Abby would have said that they are "old spirits." The dividing lines between Spiritual groups are becoming non-existent in the newborns. The Spirits coming to us that have chosen to walk in human form are far closer to the peacefulness that is our ultimate goal than previous gen-

erations. Unity has already happened in the world unseen to adult humans.

I turned my attention back to the present and felt frustrated that my family was still unable to see past my deathbed. They would remember if they would just hear me!

If you won't hear, at least open your eyes to see! Your human existence would be so much easier!

I felt the Knowing impart comfort and advice: **Relax and enjoy the journey. They will be all right just as soon as you stop struggling. You don't need that breath anymore; it is okay to let it go.**

I began to calm down and then - I felt a familiar presence.

Naomi? Is that you? I need you to guide me through this passage. You always kept me going in the right direction, and I have so many questions.

What if I miss a turn or something? What if the Ancestors don't recognize me? What if they take me for an Unaware, aimlessly wandering, and send me away?

I felt a satiny warm contentment surround me. I knew it really was all right. My journey had begun.

My mind was moving so fast. There was no pause between thoughts. I could not tell if I was moving or if it was everything else. The flow was fast yet oddly comforting. The thoughts were showing themselves in panoramic view, filled with vibrant color. The depth of detail and clarity surpassed anything I had ever witnessed.

Each time I focused on a leaf, I could feel what the leaf felt. I could smell the leaf and at the same time smell what the leaf smelled.

I realized with wonder that I was feeling color also. Pale yellow felt like a silk blanket, gently warmed by the sun. It smelled like fresh clothes on a clothes line in early spring. Blue felt light and clean and smelled pure and healthy like the charged air after a thunderstorm.

Am I the blue? The yellow? The leaf? Or are they me?

Feeling laughter well up within me, I realized that I was all these things and that all these things were me.

I am Creation, and Creation is me! There is no separation! So this is what being is! This is what Ms Abby meant!

Ms. Abby had been a wonderful life coach in a time when the term had no meaning. Thankfully, my family had known her. They had experienced her kindness and the gentle way she taught those around her the truth about the circle of life.

Ms. Abby brought her traditional Native American teachings to life by living them. She had a way of making you look at what is real in a world of smoke and mirrors. She was no guru on the mountain. There was no pretense or showboating, only truth and harmony with Creation. She was a real person who taught balance in the physical world and how to stay in tune with the Spiritual world.

It was as though Ms. Abby was nearby whispering in my ear, explaining the things as they were being revealed. Maybe it was just the familiar comfort my mind sought at this time or maybe she really was the guide that I sought in the transformation from death to life. Either way I could hear her soft voice now.

"When our Spirits take human form we agree to the joys, happiness and health that we enjoy. Those things are balanced with sorrow, pain and confusion. We agree to the hard things so that we can grow and reach the higher level of understanding that leads us closer to the peaceful beings we desire to be. We have far more control over ourselves than we like to think. It is easier to blame another than face that we are our own choices. We are not just this bundle of joy that our parents bring home and mold into well-adjusted or not-so-well adjusted adults. They do not hold our Spirits captive and distort them into repulsive or pitiful humans. We agree to the hardships that shape our character. We agree to learn how the bad things feel in order to change them."

I now realized she was much wiser than I knew. "After age 30 you no longer have anyone to blame for who you are," she would say. "You have survived childhood, adolescence, and the indulgence of your twenties. If you are a bum, that is your choice. If you are a productive member of your society, that is your choice, too. At 30 you have had plenty of time to get therapy for the things that you blame others for and move on."

Another of her teachings was more to the point. If anyone ever used their parents or other adults as an excuse for their own adult behavior, she would say, "It is your fault! You are the one who picked them! Now get on with it and find the good reasons you picked them! Take the honey from the bees, not just the sting!"

Anyone who was blessed with one of Ms. Abby's outbursts felt their inner strength restored. They also found the courage not to be victims.

It all made perfect sense now.

GY Brown and PH Jones

Chapter 2

Where is my life review? I thought that I would get a review as soon as I began the trip. What about my choices? Don't I get to make them now?

I felt anxiety overwhelm me, and I started to panic. I mentally cried out for the panic to stop and suddenly, as with the flipping of a switch, the anxiety stopped. I relaxed and felt a calm I could not explain.

Wait a minute....I get it. I am the review! Okay. Let's go back to the beginning. I really want to know if I agreed to all those extremely hard things I had to go through during my life. Ms. Abby called life our "human experience," as I remember. Was I insane or a little masochistic to have chosen that life?

Even before I could finish this thought, I saw my life begin as a vulnerable fetus struggling to form. I could hear my mother's voice coming from the bathroom of the old farm house............

"Am I finally pregnant?" wondered my mother. Tears of happiness at the thought were shining in her eyes. Having a baby was the one thing that she felt would bring completion to her life.

Hey, Mom! Here I am!!

The realization that my thoughts were heard and felt as soon as I thought them was dizzying. I was surprised that she continued to talk as though she were talking to me.

"What kind of life will you have, little one? Will you be tall like my dad or short like Luke? Will you work with your hands or your mind? Maybe you will work with both," she said gently as she rubbed her belly with a hopeful hand.

In the blink of an eye she was hanging her head over the toilet, retching violently and shedding tears of happiness. She turned her head toward my father who was holding a cool cloth to her neck and in the softest voice I had ever heard said, "We are having a baby!"

I sensed my father's joy well up in his throat with tears too thick to flow. I saw that there were some emotions that are too intense to be released. They intensify as they stay inside. I could feel the radiant hope of life emanate from every fiber of my mother's being. My father took her in his strong arms and carried her to their bed where he carefully laid her. Tears flowed down his weathered cheeks as he knelt beside the bed where he offered prayers of gratitude for her happiness. I could feel the sheer joy he felt that his precious Gracie would finally have a child. His joy, however, turned to naked fear when he remembered that he would lose her. It was in his life agreement. And he had accepted it.

His pain was so much worse than I could ever have imagined. It was like ripping flesh off with salt sticks amid screams of terror. The burning pain had a smell like nothing imagined outside of the Biblical hell. No wonder I seldom saw the light of life in my father's eyes as I grew to manhood. My father knew at that moment that he would have to lose his Gracie in order to give her what she wanted more than life itself. He had been willing to take the chance just to see the joy he was looking at now. My father would push the knowing deep inside, hoping in vain that if he did not acknowledge the pain, it would not manifest itself in real life. His Spirit knew that it would have a life of its own. The impending events would create a harshness that would govern his actions the rest of his Earthly existence.

How could I have forgotten something this important? How could I not have felt his loss and pain during my Earth walk? I would never have blamed him for his coldness. I would not have lashed out at him in anger when he seemed indifferent to my frustration. I would have understood if he had just told me!

As soon as these painful thoughts began I felt my father near, urging me to go forward in my life review. His being was one with mine, knowing what I knew and feeling what I felt. We were the completion of each other. There was no pain or guilt, only encouragement to go forward and coexist.

For weeks I struggled to grow and develop. I tried so hard not to take the life force from my mother, but she constantly infused my small being with it. Daily she would sing and talk to me, encouraging me to be whole and healthy. And all the while my father hid his pain. He knew the loss was coming. And he would never recover. His Spirit knew that his happiness was leaving with my coming. His body stayed busy working during the day and taking care of my mother in the evening. At night when he could not sleep he would go to the barn and work on the crib he was building.

I kept forming. I must have wanted to be born to these people. I remember now that I had planned to take my father's pain and emptiness away. I had planned to fill it with love and hope. How could I have forgotten?

Chapter 3

Ow! What is happening to me? I can't sense my existence clearly anymore. My being seems to be changing, maybe even becoming something different. Can this tiny body I have been building even withstand this? The pressure will surely crush it! How does anyone survive this?

A calm Knowing filled space and communicated: ***Hold on, slow down, and let the thoughts come through. Don't fight it. Billions have gone through this experience with no lasting repercussions.***

I had no idea how all this worked. Pictures began streaming by, filling all my senses. I decided I must be traveling down the birth canal but could not understand this method of becoming. It seemed to me it would be much less traumatic just to hatch. One good push, and you're out!

As I grew closer to the world into which I had agreed to be born, I began wondering if I had made the right decision.

I do not want to go out there! It looks safe and warm, and the colors are right, but it feels so sad and cold. And that noise! What is it? That can't be the soft voice of my mother making those noises – can it?

Even as the question formed, the noise stopped. Suddenly there was only silence, filled with no sound and no feeling. No thoughts whirled about making their low hum. No wishing noises came from the minds of the people present. I wondered in that moment if the planet itself was standing still.

I had not realized that the thoughts and emotions of regular humans were so powerful. I began to see and understand that thoughts form motion in the universe in much the same way as a jet moves through earth's atmosphere. I was puzzled at the sudden and complete absence of movement now.

The silence was broken then by a noise I did not understand. I did not know if I wanted to understand it. It was horrible and seemed to fill the universe with the deepest sadness I had ever felt. The pain from this noise was so thick that those near it seemed unable to breathe.

There were gasps of breath at first, then no breath at all. The high pitched whine from this pain was so shrill I covered my ears. It did not help, however, because I could still feel the pain. My ears were seeing and my eyes were feeling the all-encompassing sorrow. It smelled like rotten leaves in a dank hole and was as old as time.

This was the kind of sorrow humans always carry with them once it touches them. The stench of this kind of pain never really leaves their nostrils. This is the pain that you sense when there is sorrow behind a smile. I understood that this kind of sorrow had to be hidden. If it were allowed to show, it would steal one's breath forever. It would cripple with twisting torment, and the screams would never quiet.

Our self preservation mechanism, Ms. Abby would teach me, constantly pushes unpleasant memories into the far reaches of our consciousness to make room for our life force to grow strong and healthy. Those who walk with the conscious memory of the horrors they have seen live in a state of sorrow. It may not be that the "good die young," so much as the "sad die young." The ones who hold the sorrow the tightest succumb to its power soonest. Our life force can only push so hard for so long before it is used up. This kind of sorrow sucks the life out of us as much as abuse does. A person spends his life essence keeping it hidden from the rest of his being to protect his Spirit. He uses great life force to keep it walled up so that it can't touch the hope and goodness that balances it.

I know the source of the sorrow this day. It was that my mother had crossed to the other world that most humans can't see when they are in the state known as 'normal'. I turned and knew my mother was near offering the comfort only a loving mother can give.

Isn't it beautiful, Mom?

There were no deafening noises, only the pure tones of positive thoughts. There was no darkness, only the radiant hues of truth. This was the world where all things begin. This was the place where all truth could be kept safe, waiting to be seen and understood. This is what we forget and choose to replace with sorrow for a time. This is what we hide from while having our human experience. And this is what waits to give us rest and comfort.

I turned my thoughts back to the place of sorrow and saw the most bizarre thing so far. During my Earth walk I did not think too much about the rituals of humans. Seeing them from this vantage point painted an entirely different picture. They were moving the shell that was Mom. They were washing and dressing her as if she were going to get up and go to a party! What nonsense! How could they accept such a ritual as normal or right?

"Do not be dismayed," my mother explained in thought. "They are trying to comfort themselves. I don't need my body any more. Being without it allows me to be with you all the time.

I will be the warm breeze which will dry your tears. I will be the perfectly tuned song you hear on the wind. I will be the blue of the sky and the wetness of the river. I will be the laugh that takes your breath away.

I agreed to this a long time ago. This is how my existence changes. I decided to exist where I can always be near you and your children. You will need to take a good look now at your life agreement. Remember that you will have seven days to decide if you want this experience."

I felt my mother's calm as she settled into a restful state. She was more lifelike than I had imagined. She was just exactly like my childhood fantasies of her. She was whole, beautiful, happy and content. I felt her perfection. There were no flaws, no pain or sorrow, and no sadness or illness. She was as light as a cloud and as warm as an early summer day.

Death is not so cold, I realized as I absorbed the emotions of the moment. The only thing that is cold is the human shell without the Spirit of life in it. Mom was so happy! She seemed to know the others who were gathering around her. The tone of laughter and joy that permeated the atmosphere was intoxicating. The truth of the everlasting Spiritual connection was real and manifested itself in the complete contentment of this instant.

I turned back to my own existence, knowing that this part of my mother's journey was hers to travel now. I was happy to know she was not alone.

Chapter 4

The comfort of the moment waned and was soon replaced by sorrow as I turned my attention to the present. I became aware of a terrible sound, one which I could not readily identify. Suddenly I realized that the hideous sound was coming from my father. It reverberated throughout my entire being. The sound was so horrible, so terrible, that it created a gigantic fissure in the pattern of the human connection to the divine. I did not understand this at all.

Guidance came once more from the Knowing: *Just keep moving forward. This is part of the fulfillment of his life. He agreed to this a long time ago. There is no breath, no harm, no time, no long-lasting repercussions. It is what it is. One can not apply human aspects to Spiritual journeys.*

I gazed up into the eyes of women I did not know who peered back at me through half-swollen eyelids and lamented, "Poor little thing! What will become of him now?"

Don't you know that I am holding all the cards here? Hey! I have not decided to stay here yet. Given the way you are all acting, I am leaning toward leaving this one and taking my chances with the next offer. There is way too much sadness here. I think I might like a sunny, island home filled with pretty, happy women and proud, strong men. None of this crying, painful stuff for me! I want a life in my own giant sandbox- a sandbox where it is always sunny!

The Knowing seemed to smile at my naïveté. ***Everyone has a moment when they want their own sandbox - but only a moment. Many willingly choose a life with no sandbox at all. They choose to help others build their sandboxes. Still, they arrive at this same place.***

I was brought back abruptly to the physical world when a strange woman sensed that I was drifting away from it.

What are you doing? Hey - stop that! And stop blowing on me! I will let you know if I want your breath.

As I found myself becoming angry at this woman, I remembered Ms. Abby saying, "Sometimes we are a part of someone else's life lesson. We just kind of drift over into their story for a short period of time. Some people call it 'crossing paths.' We find later that they had a part in our story, too. At the time we just wonder why."

So this lady had to give me her breath. She had to balance an incident from the past by trying to save me. I remember the haunted look on her face. I saw that there had once been a child whom she could have saved but was too afraid to reach out to do so. She had balanced that now. So then why did she still have that haunted expression if she had corrected the incident by saving me?

I felt Ms. Abby near. "She would not allow her own Spirit to be in balance. She chose guilt instead," she explained. "Lots of folks take on the guilt of a culture because they want to be accepted by it. All that means is that they don't think they are good enough. They figure if they take on enough bad feeling, others will think they are special. It happens, for example, when a battered woman stays and raises her family. Folks say she is a good woman and call her 'long suffering.' They act as if that is a good thing. It is bull, I tell you! Nobody agrees to come here for that kind of treatment."

It was as if Ms. Abby, Mom, and others who were already gone *were* the Knowing. No wonder everyone who lived near Ms Abby never forgot her or her teachings. I began to understand why the truths she taught had been handed down for generations. This must be what she meant about the next seven generations. These were the teachings that allowed us to understand life and overcome so many of the events that devastated many families. Our foundation was grounded in true understanding without the nonsense of guilt. We learned not to take everything that happened personally, realizing that we really only have input in how we react to an event. People must live their own lives. They might project their issues our way, but we decide if we will reach out and take them inside. We knew that many of the unpleasant events that crossed our paths were not even about us.

People were back in the house now. The woman who had been sitting in the chair watching me had left the room, and another had taken her place. She was checking and changing me while the others whispered about Mom's death.

She can hear your thoughts, you know. She knows everything that you are thinking and saying no matter how quietly you whisper.

I was annoyed with them and shouted from the inside. My mother urged me to be patient. "They are grieving in their own ways. People have their own unique ways of handling things like loss. Maybe they fear that noise will rip the cocoon of sorrow they are wrapped in. If it rips maybe more loss and pain will emerge. They don't know what to do, and so they move slowly and silently, trying not to call attention to themselves. They don't want the Spirit of death to discover them. It will be a while before they remember that the death Spirit they fear is really the life Spirit they never lose. Give them their grief. It will strengthen them for the days to come."

I felt a moment of compassion for the mourners. It was time for me to observe for a while. The house remained silent, the mourners grim-faced. No one made eye contact with anyone, and I wondered if maybe they were hoping to hear from the one now on the other side.

Don't they know that she is in a painless state of comfort? I don't know why they can't just act normal.

Suddenly a nervous young girl dropped a glass. It shattered with each sliver of glass making its own distinct "ping" on the wood floor. The same old woman who had been sitting with me earlier pinched the girl's arm and sneered in a caustic whisper, "You would wake the dead."

I felt the laughter rise up in me.

Silly woman! They are not sleeping! They know everything before your mind can even think it. Wait until you remember! You will look back and wonder why you did that. Who really cares if a glass is broken?

Being physically paralyzed by infancy, I thought to myself that these people must all be crazy. None of them knew what was real. It would be less distracting to just block them all out and see what the next years would be like if I stayed.

To the Knowing I sent the thought-message: *I'll take that look at my other choices now, please.*

I began to see another life but could not tell if it was in the future or one that had already passed. It looked like an easy life with two loving parents, both happy and healthy.

Oh, I see! It is a choice! Yay! I am going to that one.

I strained a bit as I geared up to enter the life I could see.

Hey! Turn me right side up before I throw up! I have a choice here! Stop that! Why are you pushing on my chest? Get your mouth off me! Geez, what is wrong with you people? Don't you get it yet? I am the one who makes the choice, and I have not decided yet.

As I grew calm, I began to understand why people kept grabbing my infant body, pouring their own breath into it.

I think I get it. When I go to another existence, the present one must cease. So when I make the decision to go – and I see now that it is my decision – they don't understand. They try to make me stay with them because they don't see that it is my choice. That's why they turn me upside down, beat me on the back, and blow in my mouth.

I knew then that if I decided to leave this one, I would have to wait until no one was looking.

Chapter 5

It was dark and quiet when I realized that my dad was standing over my crib silently looking at me. He did not know that I was conscious and could understand his thoughts. Through his tears he said, "My son, you are all I have left. I can tell your mother is calling you to her. That must be why you stopped breathing. Gracie had an odd set of beliefs. I never really understood them. She was so sure that there were Spirits all around. She used to burn herbs for them and feel them in the air. When the wind would change she knew what it was bringing. She would say we are going to hear something. There were times when I almost believed her. When she left, there was a hard wind blowing. She looked at me and said, 'I'll wait for you on the east side of the moon, my love.'"

His voice failed him, but his thoughts continued to flow with his tears. "I did not want to believe that she was leaving. But she knew, and I guess that I always did, too."

He stroked my small, soft head with a touch that was tender and comforting. "You are so fragile - just like my Gracie. Your skin is soft like hers, too. Maybe I will call on Ms Abby tomorrow. She will know what to do if your mother is calling you to her. She will tell me what I should do and maybe make a tea so I can sleep. I will do everything I can to care for you because you are what she wanted more than life itself. I am not sure if I can give you the love a boy should have from his father. Heaven help me! I can't help but think that if you were not here, she would still be here with me. I know it is not your fault, boy. To have a child was her greatest wish - and her choice. I will try to be everything that you need me to be, and I will provide you with what you need to grow healthy and strong."

With that sobbing confession he turned to leave the room. Pausing in the doorway, shoulders bent, his back still to me, he added in a broken whisper, barely audible to me, "I promise that I will try to love you."

Then he was gone.

I saw that my father had entered a place that holds torment known only to those who have been there. No words had the power to alter the pain, and nothing could take that kind of pain away. Over time he would be able to look at the pain and sorrow and grow from the strength built from just living through it.

Ms. Abby had a few thoughts on this subject. "People think that they must say something to those who have lost someone close to them. It is something that they do for themselves because being in the presence of that kind of pain and loss is so uncomfortable," she taught. "Every living creature fears losing another close to them. The bumbling words of comfort we offer the most frequently are awkward sentiments that comfort us more than the person who is grieving."

"When people say, 'You poor thing,'" she contended, "the grieving often hear, 'I am glad that it is not me who is in this pitiful place that you are now.' When they are told, 'It is God's will' or 'They are in a better place now,' they hear, 'You have no control over your life or the people in it. You are not worthy so the choices are being made for you.' When people say, 'I know how you feel,' they would have had to experience the exact same loss with the exact same intensity. So, though most of the time they mean well, they don't know what they are talking about and would be better off saying nothing. Validating those who grieve by acknowledging the loss they have suffered and the pain which engulfs them are the only true sentiments that should really be expressed. There is no way anyone can know what other people feel, how they should grieve, or how they should move on. Silence is truth in all languages."

This would be the most emotion I would ever hear my father express. I remember that he did keep his word. He gave what he could. He loved as much as he dared. His hard exterior covered a vulnerable Spirit in constant pain. He never lived a day without the visceral nausea of loss. Every breath he took caught in his mortal fiber like a hang nail in a winter sock. He spent most of his life forcing his thoughts to the very second of existence. To look past that moment meant another moment without the love of his life. Each action was a planned movement. There were no spontaneous acts of kindness or emotion. Each stiff interchange was just a bridge to the next.

My father's life and our future relationship were defined in the moment of my mother's death.

GY Brown and PH Jones

Chapter 6

I was finally able to rest from the massive input of emotion permeating the atmosphere. Most of the people had gone and the ones who were left were silent. Now I could see and think without the distractions and vibrations of others.

So far I knew that if I stayed I could be a comfort to my father, but that I would feel unloved by him. He would be hard to understand and would seem inflexible and uncaring. If I knew that he loved me and was just having trouble expressing it, maybe I could handle that. I needed more information to make such an important decision. I thought of something that might make it easier.

I know - show me some of those heartwarming scenes that a father and son share like fishing, playing ball, going to ballgames - things like that. That will put a positive spin on this. I know there had to have been some really special times, since I did have this life.

I steadied my emotions and opened my thinking to view the scenes clearly as they unfolded. The air felt warm and the colors were crystal clear as I seemed to melt into the vision.
I saw myself sitting on the old bridge that crossed Lake Walter, kicking my feet, anxiously waiting for my father to come and show me how to fish.

I felt the hopefulness all children feel toward their parents. I had taken great care to find the perfect spot to wait on the bridge. My father would have no trouble seeing me from either direction. I waited for him, happy in the knowledge that he would surely see me, sitting there in my perfect spot, waiting for him to come. I busied myself by thinking of all the fish we were going to catch together.

The sun climbed higher in the blue sky, and still I waited. The air became hot and sticky. As I strained for any view of my father, I became aware of the fact that I was hungry and thirsty. Leaving my post briefly, I descended to the water below, watching and listening for any movement on the bridge.

I leaned down to take the cool water in my hands. As my hands slid into the still water, they created soft ripples that gently echoed outward, growing larger and longer until they splashed into the far bank.

Observing this scene from an adult view, I realized that our lives are like ripples on the water. We affect everything we touch as we pass through our human existence until we crash into the furthest bank, shattering into many droplets. At that point we become part of the bank, the water, the air, and the living things all around. It occurred to me that our lives were also like drops of water, nothing much alone but part of a much larger body that must have every drop in order to be whole.

My awareness shifted as I was startled by a shadow behind me. "Dad?" I cried out hopefully and turned around. But there was no one there. It was just the warm breeze – or was it? I left with the nagging suspicion that the shadow in the water was that of a woman, but quickly dismissed the thought. From this vantage point I could see now that it was my mother's essence. When I was there I thought it was just a shadow.

Ms. Abby's words reached across space and time once again. "That is how we humans rationalize the Spiritual presence that surrounds us. 'It is just a shadow. It is just the wind. My eyes are playing tricks on me.' When we hear something, we discount it as just something moving that we left unsecured. Maybe the change of temperature is creating that popping noise. We dismiss feelings we don't understand. We tell ourselves there is nothing more, there is no reason to explore it deeper. It was only a shadow. It is only the wind. We have just forgotten."

Disappointment settled in. It was not Dad. He was not coming. He must have had to work. Maybe he was fixing something in the garage. Maybe old Mrs. Finch had called him over to her house to fix something again. That old lady was always getting him to fix stuff. It was probably her again.

As I walked home I created reasons why he had not been able to come, vainly attempting to sooth my wounded heart and cover the loneliness that chilled me on that summer day. I realized that he was not ever going to teach me to fish. I held onto my self esteem tightly by becoming angry and thinking of all the reasons why he missed out on a really good time. I told myself that most dads would be excited to fish with their boy and decided I would just get someone else to fish with me next time. Someone who knew how much fun I was to be around.

Gradually my shoulders sagged, and I walked slowly homeward, dragging the fishing pole behind me. When I walked into the house I found him there, sitting in his chair with the newspaper in his hand. He looked at me over his horn-rimmed glasses, and I turned away without a word.

I wondered if adults knew that it is the little things they do or don't do that have lasting effects on children. Every disappointment, every delight mold a child's world view.

I hung my fishing pole on the barn wall for the last time.

Chapter 7

Well that certainly didn't do anything to encourage me to want this life! So far it is 2 - 0 for leaving this life and going to the beach! I don't think I want to go through that. Who in their right mind would? There is still just way too much pain and sorrow. Surely I picked something better and this is all a bad dream.

No, I don't think this is the life I picked at all. It looks like one disappointment after another. I seem to always be looking for someone. It appears to be full of broken promises, too. There is no reason to choose that kind of life. I am even feeling disappointed by my own choices. There has to be something that I am not seeing.

I felt Ms. Abby near. "Disappointment is an emotion that comes from internalizing our own expectations. It is painful and creates scars on the soul. It leaves us with bad feelings that often turn into bad actions. Those actions take aim at our hearts and sneak out of our subconscious at unexpected times throughout our lives, long after we forget the reason we are reacting. If we allow ourselves to remember how they feel we can avoid inflicting them on others. The chain reaction of hope we can create by eliminating unjust disappointment is one that feeds positive thought and builds self esteem.

Think how much easier it would have been if your dad had simply said he was busy that day or had taken a moment to come to the bridge to tell you something had come up. You would have been disappointed for a moment but it would not have created a scar on your soul. You would have very likely picked up that fishing pole later and perhaps even shared that activity with your own children. We can accept human nature in others just as we accept our own faults. All it takes is a little honesty and the ability to admit that we are human, too. A promise is not broken if it is changed. Both parties have to be aware of the change, however, for it to be real."

I contemplated this view of disappointment and promises. It was clear to me that communication between people could balance and heal broken promises. I recalled times I had made promises that were interrupted by unavoidable circumstances. There was always a point at which the outcome could have been changed. Making a call was not that hard. Sure, I did not like telling someone that I could not do what I had to do, but I did it. I did not have any negative residue from those changed promises because I always communicated the circumstances. Other arrangements were made by simply changing a time or place. Doing this did not leave bad feelings on either side. There were no unpleasant feelings of guilt that often affected relationships. There were no periods infused with awkwardness. Maybe there was more to this balance thing than I ever realized. I could see that things would have been better for both of us if my dad and I had communicated more effectively.

At this point I was still not sure that I wanted to continue watching this possible life. I was curious, however, to discover the reasons behind the things I had experienced. This review had brought back so many things that I had forgotten. I did not remember being an infant and making the choice to stay here. It was perplexing at this point to know that I must go back into infancy and live through all the hard points in life in order to understand the rest of my story. It seemed that I might have the power to rewrite the past by agreeing to go on from here. It was all very confusing.

I decided that I would put my confusion on hold and at least appear to move on. I would play along for now and try to have an open mind. I was not so sure that I knew the difference between what happened, what I chose, and what was going to happen at this point. Somehow it still felt lopsided and off-center.

Let's get back to the object of this review and move along to the really good parts. Show me the things that made this life unquestionably a life worth living.

In the next scene I saw Miss Johnson directing us in a school play. Everyone's parents were there to watch and take lots of pictures. I saw all the excited families and repeatedly scanned the audience for a glimpse of my dad. I had left the paper that told all about the play by the coffee pot. I knew that when he got home he would see the paper and come to watch.

The flashes of many cameras blinded me as we stepped onto the stage. I desperately hoped that I would be able to see my father when he came through the door. Time passed quickly, and soon we were taking a break. Other parents swarmed backstage around their children, bringing them drinks and cookies. Even though I was hungry, too, I spent the time searching for my dad. I was afraid to leave the stage for fear that he might not be able to find me in the crowd. I stood as tall as I could and anxiously watched for him.

Soon the others returned to the stage, and the play resumed. I continued to watch for my father, straining to see past the lights into the audience. The others recited their parts with the exacting tone people have when they recite words that are foreign to them. They sounded almost robotic in tone and expression, but I hardly noticed because the door in the back of the auditorium was opening. It had to be my father! I look hopefully but was disappointed to see it was just some kid running out the door.

I suddenly became aware that the other kids were giggling all around me. I realized with a start that they were all looking at me. I had forgotten to say my lines!! I had been so preoccupied watching for my father that I did not hear my cue!

Miss Johnson motioned for the others to continue while she gave me a scowl to make sure I understood that I just ruined her big night. I felt like disappearing. I was sure to hear about it later.

The play was almost over, and my father had still not arrived. I felt so embarrassed and alone. I felt as if my head had grown as big as the stage. It seemed to fill up the entire auditorium, becoming the only thing that people could see. At any moment I felt that it could explode and cover everything with my painful embarrassment and shame.

The other parents flooded the stage to hug and praise their children after the program ended. I slipped away unnoticed and walked home. I decided that I would confront him this time and ask him why he was not there.

The whole thing was just so unfair. Why couldn't my dad come to things with me? I was not any trouble. I always kept my room clean and helped around the house. I never asked for more allowance or brought home bad grades. I decided to tell him how I felt and how lucky he was to have such a good son.

I walked into the house armed with the words I had worked out in my head. Just as I was about to tell him how I felt, he looked at me over his dark horn-rimmed glasses with that familiar steely stare. My resolve melted away, and I mumbled only a very weak, "Good night."

Why didn't I tell him? What is wrong with just asking him why?

I escaped to my room and threw myself across my bed. I buried my face in my pillow and willed myself not to cry. As I drifted off to sleep my head started to hurt and my nose burned from stopping the tears. I refused to cry and told myself he was lucky to have a son like me.

"Was that supposed to be a good time?" I shouted at the universe. Why would anyone want to go through that? Now I would have to go to school and face Miss Johnson and the other kids. I knew I would never hear the end of it. I would always be remembered as the one who messed up the play.

Gradually my raging quieted, and through the silence came the words of the Knowing: ***This experience shaped you into the person you were meant to be. You were at every play and every game for both your personal children and those in your classroom. You made sure every child had someone there by being the missing voice for those whose parents never came.***

You were one of the first at school and were always the last to leave. You touched many lives with your smile and encouragement of lonely children. The circle of dis-

appointment picked up hope when it passed your way to become balanced. Your agreement held the promise to always make children feel wanted and to let them know that they were not alone. To do this you first had to know how it felt to be alone and disappointed.

The younger the person the more acute is their awareness of sincerity and empathy. Those you touched with hope knew you really understood how they felt and that you were truly there for them. Your own experience with pain made your compassion real. Your self esteem grew stronger. Your values came together to govern your actions toward others. Making good grades, keeping a clean room, not taking more than was yours, and most importantly helping others became morals etched into your mind at this young age. They became the principles on which you based goodness.

This moment shaped your future. It gave you the incentive to become a teacher. You knew first-hand the damage that could be caused by a self- centered teacher and a detached parent. You felt how someone could inflict emotional damage in the smallest ways just by being selfish. This event was burned into your subconscious and is what allowed you to become a caring teacher, always weighing your thoughts carefully before expressing them to your students. You made your work as a teacher extend beyond books and tests. Your classroom became a safe haven filled with the encouragement all children need to learn and feel valued. If you had not experienced these things, you would not have become the kind of teacher you were. You would not have known that scars can last for years. You would not have touched so many in positive uplifting ways that encouraged them to feel good about themselves."

I lay very still in my bed that night and pondered these things.

GY Brown and PH Jones

Chapter 8

Pondering these things proved to be somewhat intense. I still felt the pain of my boyhood trauma. But at the same time, I felt the happiness that came from knowing it had enabled me to help many of my students who experienced the same kind of pain. It was hard to keep track of what was mine eternally and what was the result of my response to these events on eternity. There did not yet seem to be a division between the two, but I felt that there must be. Somehow they merged into the same slot in the universe, much like a peg in a hole. The peg is nothing without somewhere to place it, and a hole is just empty space until the peg is placed in it. They are two very different things that become one when they inhabit the same space. The whole they create is strong and balanced.

Suddenly I felt very happy. I saw myself laughing and riding my bike with my best friend, Ross. He was always happy to see me. We had a great friendship. His mom was always drunk, and he never knew his dad. We both felt like throw-away kids. We understood each other and shared one another's burdens, as true friends always do. In addition we accepted reality in a way that children in "normal" homes never do. My vision turned to our time together.

I remembered this part of my life well. My relationship with Ross kept these memories in the conscious part of my mind unlike so many childhood memories that fade with time. We were inseparable and rode our bikes everywhere. When we weren't riding them, we were walking beside them. We were attached to them almost as much as we were to each other.

I paused to ponder that for a moment. Maybe bicycles were the best kind of friends - the kind that takes you where your heart desires and never criticizes your choice of road or path. The kind that lets you fly with the wind toward parts unknown, allowing you to feel the bumps in the road without having to deal with them directly. If a bump comes along that is too big for the bike to handle, of course, then it is you who must be the strong one and take care of you both. If the bike were damaged it would patiently wait for you to fix it and get back on. When something was after you, real or imagined, the bike's wheels fused with your body and increased speed to match your rhythm. When you paused to rest the bike patiently waited for you where you left it. Maybe I was right. Maybe a bike was the best kind of friend.

I turned back to the vision feeling the comfort of being with my best friend. We were sitting on the old bridge, tossing rocks into the water below, when I asked the question that had been plaguing me for some time. "Ross, do you ever wonder why we did not get good parents like other kids?"

Ross looked off into space and thought for a while before he spoke. "Nah, we are the kind of kids that don't need someone to take care of us. We can take care of ourselves. Besides, we don't have anyone making us come in for bed early or grounding us for low grades. Remember when that bully Rob was picking on you? Remember how me and Johnny beat the fire out of him? Johnny could not play at all for weeks after that, and he told me that his dad took a belt to him. We don't have none of that."

I thought for a minute, then said, "Yeah, but Johnny couldn't play with us anymore after that, either. Now that I think about it - there are a lot of kids who aren't allowed to play with us."

Ross made a face. "Lucas, it ain't you so much as it is me. You hang with me, and I got a drunk for a mom. Plus nobody knows who my dad is. I'm not even sure my mom knows who he is," he said wryly. "So the other moms and dads – they don't want their kids around me.

Your dad don't think that way, though. I see him watching us more than you do. I don't think that he is worried about you being friends with me. He knows that I ain't gonna hurt you or let anyone else hurt you. He keeps watch to see that nobody gangs up on us. He don't come too close 'cause he knows I can handle most anything. He's there just in case we get outnumbered or somethin'. He takes care of you, all right – just from a distance." He shrugged. "It's just his way."

Ross had been on his own pretty much his whole life. He had spent a lot of time observing people and had learned to read them pretty well. This made him wise beyond his years. He did not take it personally when other parents would grab their children and go the other way when they met him on the street. His personality did not permit the fault of others to become a part of him. He didn't realize the extent to which people discriminate against children because of their race, religion or social status. No matter how ill- mannered or cruel people were, he always thought that their negative condition was temporary.

He looked for the reasons behind their bad behavior. Perhaps it was caused by their getting up on the wrong side of the bed or the fact that they weren't feeling well that day. Perhaps they were worried or distracted. It simply never occurred to Ross that people might actually hate someone for reasons beyond their control. If Ross had a fault, it was that he thought people would care about him simply because he cared about them. I remember watching people whisper when Ross entered a room. He would be oblivious to the whispers and stares and would flash that charming smile at anyone who made eye contact with him. Perhaps Creation had given Ross the proverbial rose-colored glasses to protect him from cruelty knowing what he would suffer. I realized that Creation provides us all with a measure of comfort and gives us the tools to weather any trauma.

 I continued to mull over our friendship and bask in the warmth of what we had. Maybe I chose to take this life so that Ross would have a friend to watch over him in ways he could not see. Perhaps there was more to the past lives theory than I realized. Maybe we had been brothers in another life. The thought seemed so familiar that I wanted to explore it further.

 How could we possibly forget a thing like that? Had we been separated too soon and then been sent here to complete the things that we were unable to learn from each other? Maybe we needed to fulfill an agreement that we had not had time to finish.

 Now that I thought about it, there were many people who felt familiar during what Ms Abby called my "Earth Walk." There were places that felt familiar, too - like I had been there before. I wondered if the notion of DÉJÀ VU was viewed as a mystery just so people would hesitate to explore it further. Western culture had a tendency to avoid anything that was unknown. Seems that it may be yet another way society derails us from knowing too much about our remembering.

Chapter 9

Apparently we spend a lifetime forgetting our former selves. In the culture I had been viewing, at least, the focus was definitely on forgetting. Life would be so much simpler if we could retain the knowledge and understandings that we came here with. If we could know the things to which we agreed, it would make life much more pleasant. Wouldn't things be a lot easier? Even if there were some really hard times, we would be able to see past them.

It seems to me that there would be far less depression and anger - far fewer mental disorders, too - and times when we wonder who we really are. We would just release it and move on. I wondered who made up these rules and who it is who makes us forget. Why else would we forget answers that could make life easier?

The answer came from the Knowing: *You do know all these things when you are here. They are part of your genetic memory, housed in every cell of your being. The tiniest part of you holds the memory of all things you encountered before. There are very few who remember how to access the part of the mind where Sacred knowledge lives. Some work for years to accomplish the task of remembering. Some pay others to help them remember, and some try to force others to do it for them using human ploys like guilt or pride.*

Many find it easier to follow those who pretend to know the answers. Some look to those who demand that people pay homage to them. They find it easier to believe that in exchange they will take care of the hard stuff that would require thinking on a Spiritual level.

Some claim to be the voice of God. Others claim to be the only ones who can hear that voice. Still others find it easier to buy into the agreement of others by following their lead.

But most people are simply paralyzed by their own fear. They are unable to access their own centers. Sometimes fear is carefully placed by zealots and governments to control the masses of people who are seeking understanding and are drawn toward an enhanced existence. They do it deliberately in order to control them.

The common thread tying them together is that they are all searching. All those who do not remember spend their lives seeking answers to explain who they are, where they come from, why they are here, and where they are going.

That sounds pretty simple. But do we ever remember? How do we get past the obstacles, some of which are carefully and deliberately placed to misdirect us? How do we know what is ours and what is someone else's?

To know any of the answers, you must learn to be quiet and listen to the voice which connects you to the divine. It is the same voice that you came here with. Many people find they can do this through meditation and relaxation. Some cultures encourage their young to remember from the beginning.

Absorbing all this information was easy from my vantage point. I was not consumed with work or trying to raise a family and keep up appearances. How did anyone have the time or energy to encourage their children to remember while they were teaching them to be socially acceptable?

I did not understand why the Western culture I had been viewing - and that I had obviously experienced - worked so hard to make us forget and become something else. It appeared that all civilized cultures do this. It looked like what I knew as third world countries were the ones who did not focus on social standing and material possessions. They seemed to actually encourage their children to know the past and the future by living in a knowing present, one which included remembering.

Children are not schooled in every culture to work for a system that allows little room for a personal Spiritual existence. They are encouraged to maintain their Spiritual connection at all times. Dominant Western culture does not encourage people to be themselves and live as individuals. Everyone must stay within their social and financial station for the comfort of those who consider themselves to be advantaged. They must be the worker ants carrying money and synthetic prosperity to those who have convinced others that they are of this advantaged class. They convince the worker ants that to be moral or "good" they must not deviate from the pattern.

This ruling class sees that the pattern is physically appealing and are rarely interested in taking a deeper look. To deviate from the pattern would bring turmoil and doubt to the masses. It would make them question what is real and what is not. Socioeconomics are designed to rule not just Wall Street but also Main Street. Thoughts which fall outside the boundary of political correctness are often labeled 'corrupt' and 'immoral,' al-

lowing Guilt to control and stifle them through the desire to be accepted. Remove the pattern and the Guilt, and people are free to think for themselves and hear that Spiritual voice that shouts within them. They would be able to hear the voice that brought them here.

The ones who remember are those who can smile with stomachs distended in hunger. They are those who face each day without carrying the scars of the torments they have suffered at the hands of other human beings. They are the ones who have the light of an old Spirit shining in their eyes - the ones who always have a kind word or smile for someone else. They know that this is only a passing phase their Spirit is going through to learn and understand. They live with the knowledge that their Spirit is tethered to the divine through space and time, not by the trappings of modern society.

I could not help but think that if I had been able to access this knowing during my human experience, these memories would have greatly enhanced my life. My human experience would have been more fulfilling. I would have been happier!

There would not have been all those times where I felt like nothing because of something someone else did or did not do. Given the chance I think I would have chosen a whole different culture - a culture that allowed a person to carry the knowledge of all eternity with them while walking this Earth. How much richer life would be if we understood the control we have over our own destiny. There would be no need to fill up our empty lives with possessions and money. There would be no empty places that filled with sadness, loneliness or bitterness. There would be no guilt governing our actions. We would be free to walk in beauty through the rocky parts of life never feeling the sharpness or coldness of the rocks.

I wondered if crime would exist at all if humans were encouraged and taught to maintain their connection to the divine. There would be no need to steal because we would possess everything we needed. There would be no need to kill since we would know that we are all part of one Creation. We simply would not want what others have since we would have all that we agreed we would have. We would not act out of guilt because we would be guiltless. There would not be any strife because we would all be living in oneness and beauty.

What a wonderful place it would be. If only we could remember.

GY Brown and PH Jones

Chapter 10

Seeing my friendship with Ross in review had made this choice of lives more attractive. I turned my attention back to infancy for a while to rest and consider what I had seen before moving on. This stage of physical existence was particularly difficult because no one could understand me. I usually just gave up and screamed for a while. The indignities were tremendous. The lack of control over everything was irritating. I wondered if any of the adults feeding me had ever tasted the food they were giving me. If they had known how it tasted then it would have been no mystery to them why I threw up most of it.
An unknown woman was messing with me again.

Where is my dad, and why isn't he doing this? It would be a whole lot less embarrassing if he would just take care of these things. Then I wouldn't have these strange women cleaning me up and clucking about how pitiful I am. Keep up this humiliating stuff, people. I am still deciding and have a little time left.

I realized that I must back away from this physical view in order to see clearly without the sympathetic clucking and human interference. I decided to return to the visions of my life so that I could escape the indignity
I had already been shown that I would be blessed to have Ross as my friend for life. We survived childhood

somehow. The cruelties inflicted by other children on us were not so bad compared to what some kids went through. I could see that both Ross and my dad shielded me from many harsh and harmful events.

As it turned out, Ross and I went to college together where we both met the loves of our lives. We married in the same year. Ross loved Sally with the same intensity that I loved my beautiful Naomi.

I worried about Ross for a while after his mom died. Even though she was never like a real mom who cooked or anything, she was his mom. When she died Ross was lost. He did not know what to do without having to take care of her. He started going out and partying a lot. I thought that he might end up like his mom after all.

One night we were at a party when a fight broke out. Ross's date bolted for her car, and Ross ran after her because she was really drunk. She did not see him as he ran to stop her and hit him with her car. Man, he was in bad shape for a while. We did not know if he was going to make it. He carried the scars from that night the rest of his life. I asked him one day if he minded them. He said, "Naw, kid. Those scars on my face make me look tough. Besides, now my face matches my insides - all scarred up".

It would be a long time before I understood what he meant by that. Ross was an old soul in a damaged body like so many people who are truly wise. He could see things for what they were. He knew how feelings are hurt and how to heal. He saw past the external appearance into the heart of many a man. He absorbed pain and transmuted it into a smile.

He could calm a storm with his cock-eyed grin and twinkling eyes. Anyone viewing Ross on the outside would think that he had always had it made. They would think that he never had a care in the world and that he had been born with the proverbial silver spoon in his mouth. Only those who really knew him knew that Ross had been made strong by holding the world on his shoulders for a very long time. I could not have survived childhood without him. His friendship was certainly reason enough to choose this life.

Wait - what? Don't show me that again! Change it!

I suddenly remembered that I had lost Ross too soon. I felt like I was running but not gaining any ground - as if the universe had seized control of my review. The scenes unfolded, taking on a life of their own. I saw Ross coming home with that cockeyed grin, whistling that silly tune with his hands full of flowers for Sally. He had seen them in an abandoned lot on his way to work that morning. It really was a beautiful bouquet of deep red Iron Weed, purple Pop Eyed Joe, and Goldenrod. His normal caution was lost in the image of Sally's smile so he did not notice when a young man turned to follow him.

I felt panic grip every fiber of my being. Surely the power of the vision must also have the power to change what was about to happen! Ms Abby always said that we are not given visions to torture us but so that we can change something to bring about a positive outcome. And I knew I had to change this!

"Ross, turn around!" I heard myself scream. The picture was suddenly moving like a jumpy old black and white film. The colors were gone.

"Why can't I change this?" I screamed inside my head.

I felt the voice of the Knowing but wanted to shut it out. I already knew the answer and did not want to hear it: *It already happened. You are just an observer. You do not have the power to change something that already happened.*

What could I have done to change this terrible moment? There had to be something that I had missed - a clue – something! Maybe I could have delayed him somehow or picked him up that day. There had to have been something that I missed!

The Knowing continued: *His story was written long before he shared this life with you. There is no need to beat yourself up. There is no need for you to feel guilty. His life was his choice. The only choice you ever had was if you would share a part of your life with him.*

The mugger would take all he had on him – only ten dollars - then stab him in the stomach.

This can't be what happened! This has to be one of those choices I have yet to make. Why else would I be seeing this? This must have been one of those scraps he was always getting into. He recovered from all of those. That has to be it.

The metallic smell of blood filled the air as I watched the life seep out of my beloved friend. Slowly the finality of the moment sank in. I surrendered to the numbness of complete and utter shock and disbelief. I could not move.

I just wanted to know why. Why would I want to have a best friend for all those years only to lose him when we were finally happy? That is just not fair. I saw all the good times we had and how much we helped each other get through life as a couple of misfits. Ross taught me what unconditional love was. He gave me hope and showed me how to trust. No matter how moody or mad I was, Ross was the same. No matter how many times I really screwed up, Ross was the same. No matter how big a mess I got in, Ross was there to help me clean it up.

Why would I have chosen to know and lose him? Was it worth it?

Even in my state of shock, I knew the answer was yes.

Chapter 11

I saw next that I was sitting with my wife. We were in our home. I realized that it had been hours since I had spoken when I looked into Naomi's lovely face. The worry had etched lines around her dark brown eyes. For days we had been dealing with the arrangements for Ross's funeral and taking care of his wife and little girl. Arrangements. What kind of word is that anyway? Arrangements are bouquets of flowers or placements of furniture. So can we pick what kind of arrangements we want to make for someone we love who has died? If that were so I would pick the arrangement in which Ross was still with us. I dared not speak of the things that were going through my mind for fear that Naomi might think she had married a loon. "Let's get it over with," I heard myself say.

The funeral director came over and reached out his cold hand. I wanted to resist the hand shake but realized that I was expected to act in the accepted manner. As he mumbled all the appropriate condolences, I thought I detected a hint of a smile on the side of his thin, pale mouth. I had the urge to reach over and bust his mouth so that the grin was even and his lips had some color. One well placed punch and he might look more human. At least he would have had some life to the mouth that was forming words he did not mean. It was clear – at least to me - that we were just another grieving family to exploit.

I felt Naomi's hand on my arm. "Lucas, we need to make a decision. Sally cannot do it at this point. It is up to you." I looked to the chair where Sally was sitting and knew Naomi was right.

I went on auto pilot then, going through the motions of picking out a box to hold the shell that once held Ross's beautiful spirit. I closed my mind when the salesman commented, "He will be very comfortable in this one." I didn't trust what I would say or do if I allowed myself to really comprehend his ridiculous words.

Tears welled up from my soul at the loss of my one true friend. I was half expecting Ross to jump from behind the velvet curtain saying, "Gotcha, dude" any second. The thought of that made me smile through my tears. He would never stand for us to be this sad.

I looked at the others and realized that they were all looking at me. I missed my cue again, I decided. I must concentrate more on my acting. There must be another decision to make. I delivered my next line, "I'm sorry. I was lost in thought. What was the question?"

The funeral director repeated the question, "Will that be cash or charge?" I stared at him for a moment, then walked away to gain my composure.

Out of habit, I found myself running it by Ross. "What do you want me to do, buddy?"

Ross's answer was very clear. "Go cheap, dude, so the worms can finish fast. Don't want that meal to last forever, ya know. Besides, I need you to take care of the wife and kid. Save the funds for that."

My tears returned as reality began to sink in. He really was gone. The pain of losing the one person who knew me inside and out was too great. I saw the man I was on his knees sobbing in the dark parking lot of that funeral home. The sadness that echoed from the sobs poured out into the universe causing visible ripples in the fabric of

Creation. I had seen sadness like that before. I had heard it clearly in an old farmhouse long ago. Now I knew what it felt like. I understood that the sorrow would be with me forever.

Even the sadness did not make the moment completely real. There must be a point when our minds go to a place of safety. We seek the surreal to survive until our brains can process the information in front of us. I turned my attention toward others affected by the sorrow. I saw Ross's wife holding the hand of their little girl at his funeral. She turned toward me with only a blank stare. The energy of life was hovering near but it did not seem to touch her. All emotion was drained from her. It was hard to be sure that it was even Sally. The constant smile and cute dimple were gone. Those snappy green eyes that sparkled with laughter were dull and lifeless. I felt it then in my very soul. Ross really was gone.

Hours or maybe it was days later, I saw us all standing around a wooden box suspended over a hole in the ground. The minister was standing at one end of the box mumbling something about green pastures, no pain, and gold streets. He wore a serious look on his face and glanced at those of us who stood nearby. I wondered if he was looking to see if we looked sad enough.

I didn't know how it worked exactly, but I found myself wondering how anyone could be a minister or a funeral director. It seemed to me that they actually made a living from the grief and sorrow of others. They console and comfort, but would they do so if there was no money to pay?

We left the cemetery wondering how we were going to go on without this man. Life would have been much easier to survive with Ross as my companion. We could have taken our families on vacations together like we planned. My children could have had the best Uncle in the world. But he was gone.

My head, neck, and shoulders ached that night as I lay beside my sweet Naomi, realizing that I had knowingly and willingly taken on the responsibility of my best friend's wife and child as well as my own. Did I really decide to do this? This is not the joy of life I would have chosen. It was way too hard and filled with too much sorrow.

Chapter 12

I was lost after Ross died. I remembered that now. I neglected my wife at a time when she needed my support. I realized how selfish I had been and that my selfishness had caused pain to the one I loved most.

Guilt. How can such a small word carry such a huge impact? It is a heavy burden carried by mankind, a sadistic wheel of our own creation. There is no way of getting off the wheel because if we do, we will feel guilty about getting off. And that puts us right back on. We run on the wheel, going faster and faster, until we can't run any more. Falling off in exhaustion we find that we do not even have the energy to care. And for a time Guilt rests. We lay our emotional selves beside the wheel and cry out for it to have its final revenge.

We eagerly watch to see if Guilt will carry out the murder of the source. We wait with slumped shoulders and hollow eyes. We wait until we realize that it had no power of its own. It only had what we gave it. Once we step away from the Guilt and begin to feel again, we vow never to climb back on that wheel. Sometimes we are strong enough to stay off. Sometimes we are not.

My vision shifted, and feelings rushed in like a wind shear on a steep mountain slope. I felt like it was pushing my head down into my body. I began to fall from the weight, tumbling head over heels until I crashed into something substantial enough to stop me.

Naomi! How could I have caused you so much pain?

I heard the screams of agony coming from the delivery room as I rushed toward the closed door. I entered the room to see my beautiful Naomi bathed in sweat and in tremendous pain.

Why did I want a child? What if she dies like my mom did?

Just then I realized I had been haunted by Fear for nine months. It was not just the loss of my friend. It was Fear in its rawest form, the kind of Fear that chills your bones just by being in the same room with it. You shiver uncontrollably as its spiny grip tightens. It is the kind of Fear that conjures up images of underworldly places, throwing visions of faceless beings into the corners of your visions.

This kind of Fear was a thing, not an emotion. It enters your dreams and makes you wake up screaming. It is so real in that you are not sure if you are screaming out loud or just in your mind. It increases your heart rate until you hear your heartbeat in your ears long after you sit up. The sound gets louder and the pounding harder until you wonder if you are having a heart attack.

Fear is strong enough to change our thoughts and reactions. It can even make us turn away from the love of our lives and doubt the truths we know inside. Viewing from this angle, I was in awe of its power. I asked the Knowing how something so painfully destructive could live inside of us.

I felt the low vibration I had come to recognize: **Fear is not an emotion of our own Spirits. It is a tool used by humans to control other living things. We are** *taught that when bad things happen to us it is because of something we have done or because there is a lesson for us to learn. As children we are told that if we do something bad, we will be punished. This creates a place for Fear to be born and grow. We avoid doing bad things because we Fear the unknown punishment. The punishment we imagine is usually far worse than the reality because we allow Fear to feed it. To inflict Fear on other living things is as damaging as inflicting prejudice. It is never forgotten and grows stronger with age.*

I rushed in and saw Naomi looking with wild eyes at the man she loved with all her heart. It was clear just how cold and distant I had become, especially with Naomi. I had granted Fear life, and it had grown strong by feeding off of my Spirit.

Naomi could feel and see the realization I had experienced. Her eyes told me she understood. There was no air between us. We were one Spirit sharing the same knowing. Our breath came and went in unison with the universe. We shared the same consciousness in this moment. I realized that she knew in the same way generations before her knew. I felt the power of a mother's knowing.

Naomi's gaze held the resolute glint of a mother bear. I recognized that look for I had seen it on occasions when a threat had come near our child or our family. I appreciated the power of the protective nature of motherhood. It is a force that strikes fear and awe in the strongest of beings. Only a fool would mess with that!

"Lucas! It's time. I'm so glad you are here! Now - let's have this baby!"

Taking her by the hand, I looked into her eyes and thought, "She is just like my mother. She knows things." And she did.

Chapter 13

Our daughter Marissa Grace came screaming into a cold, brightly-lit world completely surrounded by love and hope. I promised that she would have a loving and caring father all of her days and that I would make her mother the happiest woman in the world. I vowed to take care of them and protect them from any harm that might try to visit them.

As the nurse laid my precious baby girl in my arms, I knew what life and love were all about. I had never held an infant before, and the feeling completely overwhelmed me. The smell, feel, and sight of her radiated unconditional love. I encountered for the first time in my life pure, uncorrupted trust.

This little life trusts me completely not to hurt her. In my hands I am holding the embodiment of Creation.

This is the moment we are driven to know and feel as our bodies morph into adults. The rage of adolescent hormones wakes the sleeping giant that will become a parent who will protect his young at any cost. The strength of our Ancestors becomes ours to thrust our genetics forward.

I heard the understanding and felt the comfort of life ongoing. It dawned on me that at that moment I was in the same position that all who had come before me were in at one time. This sameness bonded me to the prehistory men about whom we know so little. The sameness bonded me with the other parts of Creation, too, that procreate and evolve.

So this is the true connection to our Ancestors - knowing that we breathe the same air, drink the same water, and hold our newborns with wonder.
This is the embodiment of the pure love the Creator has for each of us. All of Creation is represented in this one tiny body at this one moment in time. This is the cycle of life in its true form.

As I was lost in the miracle of the moment, I felt an unfamiliar warmth covering my hand. I looked down and laughed as I realized that my beautiful baby had just wet on me! Once again I was reminded of life's balance. My daughter had just managed to balance the warm, cozy envelope of innocence with a nice, wet dose of reality!

Chapter 14

It seemed that I had already made some commitments to this world and the people in it. I had taken them as my own in my heart, and I knew their weaknesses and fears. I knew how to put them at ease and how to help them feel secure.

How does this work, then, if I decide not to stay? Do they go on to have lives with another husband and father? Will Ross's wife and daughter have someone else who will take care of them? How does this work if I am not to feel guilty about my life agreement? How do I know that they will be all right if I choose not to stay?

Answers began coming to me before my questions were finished. ***The others have to make their own choices, independent of you. They may choose to agree or not to agree to the life that is shown to them at a specific time. They might wait and pick another at a different time or they might choose to be a part of your vision and life. Either way you do not have the authority to decide for anyone other than yourself.***

They might make a decision based on something that they will see in your life agreement. Or it might not have anything to do with you. As a human you tend to think that everything around you is about you. This is a dangerous and untrue assumption. More times than not

the events in which you are involved have little to do with your choices and more to do with those of others. Sometime during your agreeing to your life, you also agree to being a part of another's life agreement. You might agree because of a past life involvement with another person. Maybe there was a life sharing between you and this person. Maybe there was unfinished business in another life. Either way, interaction can only happen when both parties agree. Don't try to make it all about you.

So we really do have a choice in how we live, what we do, and how we allow life to impact us? How sad that most of us do not know that we were given a choice. We don't remember that the things that happen to us are the result of our own choices. We blame others for our unhappiness. We act as though we are victims in our own lives when nothing could be more untrue. How uncomplicated and content life could be if we could remember these things!

Maybe the unfairness in life comes from our forgetting. That would certainly be an area where we can place the blame. Who forces us to forget?

Immediately I felt a jolt backwards almost like a giant hand had grabbed my shirt collar. I realized that I was afraid. And that little bit of Fear was enough to block my understanding.

Forgetting is also a choice, Lucas. While it is true that adults in this culture encourage forgetfulness, they do not make you forget. You agree to it. People in many other cultures do not live by the forgetting. They know that their children chose the families with whom they would share life, and they honor that choice. Your culture may be the dominant one in your mind, but it is not the only culture or the only place to have a life experience. The arrogance of your culture is the biggest barrier between truth and fantasy. It is so massive that most of your kind never try to look past it.

The glimpse you had at the whole picture through the eyes of your Native friend Abby brings understanding within your reach now. It has nothing to do with your circumstance in life. She knew that Naomi was a descendant of a people who still hear the Ancestral voice of truth and would understand. It was Abby's choice to help the members of your family have an understanding of the true life experience. Everyone agreed to share their lives with each other. Naomi brought with her much knowledge and a deep understanding of the truth.

That changed things a bit for me. Yes, we are a part of the divine and Creation, but only to a point. It will go on without us. We can be a part or not and still not have any real influence on other parts. I got it now. Thinking about all the times I felt as though I was watching my life rather than being in my life made me realize that it just wasn't all about me. All the surreal events that swirled around me were not about me either. I was just a character in someone else's play. I was willing to play the part while they "got it."

Why do we have to suffer so that others can learn their lessons? Why can't they just get a clue and know what is right without involving us?

The now familiar Knowing seeped into my understanding from within. I vaguely wondered when it had become a part of me and not something communicating with me.

On some level you agree to be a part of their lessons. They do not have the authority to involve you without your consent. Maybe it teaches lessons that you have not learned yet. Maybe it gives you the opportunity to correct a mistake by repeating the same scenario. It could be that there are things that you are trying to understand by playing all the parts.

There are some teachings that say that in order to understand all things, you must be all things. If you are abused in one life it is likely that you were the abuser in another, the observer in the next, and the one who stops the cycle of abuse in yet another.

Walking in the shoes of another is only part of the understanding. You must also see it from the outside looking in while feeling it but not touching it. You have to be the one to balance the situation. There are four ways of experiencing a situation before you can understand it. It is no different than the other parts of life where four is the complete picture - the four phases of life, the four seasons, the compass directions, sacred winds and so on. Life is circular rather than linear. There is more to it than being born at point "A" and dying at point "B". Life is not attached to the physical bodies you walk around in.

Many times you will encounter people who are greatly destructive. They go around with chips on their shoulders just looking for someone to knock them off.

They try to create problems where none exist, perpetuate lies and chaos, and work overtime to make sure others are all in a dither. Much of the time we see them playing the 'woe is me' game. What they are really doing is hiding behind the 'woe' while the 'me' wreaks havoc. Maybe they are trying to renege on their promises by constantly blaming others for their problems. They foolishly think that they are not accountable for failing to keep their promises.

Others find that they get more attention by being needy. They feel that they get more from others that way. Some even think that they can get others to do what they came here to do. Some go through life interfering in others' life agreements. As long as they are doing this, they don't have to face their own.

Ultimately everyone will face his or her own agreement. People will answer for what they did or did not do. If they decide that they no longer want to be a part of their current life and kill themselves, they have only resigned themselves to come back and start the process over. The same life will happen as the agreement was made no matter how many times they have to restart. Suicide is not a way out - only a way to send one back to the start position.

Many do keep going back to experience the same issues over and over. Often it seems that they may never get it right, and maybe that's part of their agreement. It is hard for most sane humans to understand that there are some who just want to be in pain, turmoil, and danger. They thrive on chaos, paranoia, Fear, and hopelessness. Some might say that they are sent here to show what the other side is so that people know what not to do. The one truth in all of these assumptions is that somewhere in your agreement, you agreed to be a part of the insanity and will learn from it.

The old adage that says you can't love anyone unless you love yourself is true in the life agreement existence also. If you have chosen to find fault with yourself, you are not living up to your promise and are using hate to alter or control your promise. There is no way that you can carry through your agreement if you are focused on self-loathing. Blaming others for the way you are is another cop out to your own promise agreement. Point your finger at others long enough and you will lose sight of where you are. You need to remember that while you are pointing at others, you are sending daggers into your own being, causing emotional leakage. Emotional leakage is not plugged by others. It is an open drain on your psyche, mind, Spirit, and emotional self. As you concentrate your energy on plugging the hole, it sucks in others to give more energy to the unending flow. Ultimately you wither as those around you realize that the hole can't be plugged.

Those who are constantly wanting what others have are never satisfied either. The richest one is not the one that has the most but is the one who needs the least. Your life agreement really isn't all that hard. It is, after all, what you agreed to do. The universe would not have allowed you to make one that was not do-able. The problems come when we stall, change our mind, or attempt to interfere with the agreements of others.

Chapter 15

I am one with The Knowing. I am a droplet in the sea of everything that was, is, and will be. I did have this life. I chose this life experience. I see clearly that this was my life. Those were the people with whom I chose to share life, and those were the things I agreed to do. My sorrow was balanced with happiness. This was my life, my choice.

My life with Naomi was a happy one. Sally lived with us, and we settled into a routine that worked well for all of us. Sally was quiet, seldom showing emotion. She never recovered from Ross's death and spent the rest of her days waiting until she finished here so she could go and join him. She was a big help to Naomi, especially with another child on the way, and went about quietly doing household chores.

Sally's and Ross's little girl was a great source of comfort to us all. So much like her father, Lyndee Rose was full of life. Most nights we could hear her in her mother's room, acting out her school day. Sally seldom responded to the drama before her, but Lyndee just tried harder. All Lyndee's plays ended with, "I love you, Mommy." It seemed that little Lyndee's life agreement consisted of taking the pain of others - starting with her mother.

I am glad that they lived with us. Naomi and I were able to be there for Lyndee in ways her mother just couldn't. We took pictures at her plays and swooped her in the air just for fun. She played with Marissa and was the loving older sister she adored. They were like sisters in every way except blood. Lyndee was an old soul just like her dad had been and was wise beyond her years. In fact, I often found myself asking her the questions that I would have asked Ross if he had been there. Her answers often sounded exactly as his would have sounded.

I had forgotten how happy Lyndee was as a child, before the illness took a part of her joy and riddled her body with pain. I had often questioned why it seems that people who are the most intuitive and available to others - the healers and comforters - have to cope with illness and sadness more than those who are only concerned with their own well being.

I heard the merged voice of my Spirit and the Knowing explaining how my generation had opened the path for the children to come to know without having to suffer abuse.

It takes strife to tone intuition just like it takes exercise to tone and strengthen muscles. Most humans don't do anything they don't have to do. They don't have an intuitive reason for acting on anything that does not bring them pleasure. Strife and emotional pain are exercises for intuition. They sharpen understandings in all creatures.

I had watched the sensitivities in emotionally abused children grow fast and strong, much more so than in those who basked in the love of their families all of their lives. I had seen it in my students, and I had seen it in Ross.

These children always have intuitions that are heightened above those who grow up in emotionally-nurturing homes. Basic survival instincts kick into overdrive in the abusive home. These children's survival depends on their being able to sense the moods of those around them. They learn very quickly to foresee the reaction of the adults to stimuli and vary their behavior accordingly.

Children who do not have parental nurturing always look for it in their adult relationships. That is why we often see people remain in abusive relationships even if it gets them killed. One disturbing behavior found in the less aware is that the abused becomes the abuser in an attempt to balance the unjust events they suffered. Abusers also seem to have heightened intuitions. They are heightened for the same reason- they develop them for survival. They forgot that they agreed to the abuse for a more noble reason. Maybe the reason was to right a wrong from another existence or balance another part of their lives.

There is only so much perfection allowed each of us. We all must have something to help us grow. Many times those who have no financial concerns have an ailing child, or those who have the fewest resources have the happiest homes. Balance will happen. It is the natural course of life. All things level out. We see examples of this all the time. It is easy to understand them in nature. A long hot summer is followed by a cold winter. A bumper crop of fruit one season may be followed by a season with no fruit at all. A time of great happiness and comfort is often followed by a period of trials and problems. We see a family that goes for years without losing any members. Suddenly they will have numerous deaths and illnesses. Someone who has enjoyed an extremely healthy life will suddenly have many physical problems.

The children who understand that they are chosen for higher service and that the abuse is part of the balance often develop physical limitations, autoimmune disorders and other stress-related diseases. Usually as their illnesses progress their abilities as healers and seers increase. The amount of pain and hurt they take from others may pass through them but it always leaves a trace on its journey. When we encounter these people we must not feel sympathy for them but honor them as warriors of creation.

Lyndee's early onset arthritis and cancer later in life were by-products of her ability to bring pure joy to others in the face of her fruitless search for parental nurturing. Though Naomi and I did what we could, Lyndee was there to watch us with our own children and recognize there was a difference. She saw what she was not able to get from her own mother.

Lyndee never gave her cancer a life of its own like so many cancer patients do. To her it was just part of her life agreement. Her ability to know from a distance when one of her loved ones needed her help was part of her ability to tune into the higher vibrations available to those who are living their agreement. That is why we see some who are truly noble in the face of adversity and pain. The ones who are well adjusted do not blame anyone for their suffering and know that they will gain much understanding on the other side of the pain. They know that there are things they must suffer in order to complete their agreement by truly knowing what it feels like to be hurt or sick. They can easily forgive because they know that the agreements were made long before a transgression was committed. They know that the hurtful things that others do are seldom personal but are acted out in an effort to compensate for their own shortcomings.

The newest generation of children are coming with knowledge and understanding that will not be lost. They will survive the probing and diagnosing of my generation. We had to label children we saw as "different" so that we could treat something we did not understand. We pigeonholed children, placing them into categories in an attempt to explain why they were "different." Of course they are different! They are supposed to be different!! They remember!! And they will kindly look at our ignorance with understanding laced with pity and move on unaffected.

But are the understandings we have when we come here enough to carry us through and to maintain an enlightened life. Were they there all along?

The understandings are always with you. The society in which you live often changes and shapes what you know on a conscious level. Remember, some cultures teach their children to forget. Not only are they encouraged to forget their agreements, but they are also discouraged from staying connected solidly to Creation. Few parents are secure enough in who they are to allow their children to continue to communicate with an unseen Creator. On a subconscious level they view this connection as adversarial.

One of the rare times when children are allowed to remember this connection is when they are physically ill. Usually they are left in their beds with no pressure to do anything other than get well. Parents often make promises during these times which involve the spirit in return for the health of the child. They agree to let the child be more in the Spirit - which should be where they are anyway. They leave the child alone to dream and remember. This carries over into adulthood.

When people become feverish they often become delirious. When they are delirious they see things and hear things that leave them wondering if the dream was real or not. Are they just closer to their true selves and to creation because their defenses are low and social pres-

sure is off? "It seemed so real," they say. But soon, they typically rationalize it away by saying something like, "I had some weird dreams while I was sick."

    I must have chosen to stay and be a happy father, loving husband, and a best friend. I must have chosen to keep my knowledge. After seeing what I had seen in review, I knew I had chosen wisely.

Chapter 16

Yes, this was the life I had chosen. Reviewing it made me realize that I had chosen well. There was a balance, as there must be in every life experience, of the good and the bad. But the good was so totally worth whatever it took to balance it out! The constant through it all was the love of my family. My love for my wife and children ran strong and deep as I strived to be the father I had never had.

Being motherless in the physical sense created a void that could have been filled, at least in part, by my father. Unable to do so, the void deepened by a distant father motivated me to be there not only for my own daughters but for Ross's as well. It is what drew me to the field of education and is why I became a teacher. It is also the reason that I remained in the classroom for over thirty years. The extra money I could have made as an administrator tempted me many times, but I could never quite bring myself to leave the children. I loved having the opportunity to build relationships with them and to teach them to trust again. In many ways, I was happiest when I was in my classroom with my students. They were all my children and remained so for the rest of my life.

Nothing gave me more pleasure than to see one of my former students in town or have one of them drop by the school where I taught. I wanted my classroom to be a home for them, especially for those who, like me, were not afforded the opportunity to have a nurturing relationship with a parent. In my years as an educator, I was a father figure to many. And I loved that.

All children are gifted. That had been my creed for thirty years. I had not hesitated to voice my opinion about the matter, either, in faculty meetings and in the teacher workroom. As far as I was concerned, there was no need for special programs for those who were labeled "gifted" by the system. My position did not endear me to those who worked in the special gifted and talented programs, but I didn't care because I knew I was right. I worked hard to help each of my students discover his or her area of giftedness. So I took notice when I began to see children who seemed to have new and very different gifts. It was most apparent in my own home where I could observe some of these new gifts first hand in my own children and Ross's daughter. I loved to sit and watch them at play, realizing that playing was their work.

One day when Marissa and Lyndee were very young, I was watching them at play when I noticed that they were not talking very much. This seemed odd to me as most of the children I had known talked pretty much nonstop. As I studied them in the days that followed, I discovered that they communicated very well – only without using any words.

I remembered that Ross and I were so close that we could finish one another's sentences. Our girls seemed to be taking this a step further. Was this a new gift I was seeing? And if so, were other children similarly gifted? I began to closely observe the girls' friends when they came to visit, and I found that there were indeed others gifted in this same area of nonverbal communication.

When Lyndee started to school, we worried that Marissa would be lost without her. That proved not to be the case, however, because Marissa amused herself with her imaginary friends. She would play with them for hours, laughing and talking about all sorts of things. Evidently she was able to hear them, too. Naomi would smile quietly and say that she was playing with the Little People who were part of her Native American heritage. She and Marissa even made little toys for them.

Whether they were real or imagined, I couldn't say. What I could say was that Marissa was always happy and never alone. She told me when she started to kindergarten that her friends at school had imaginary friends, too, but that they had to be kept secret from their parents. When I asked her why, she said simply, "They are afraid. They don't understand like you and Mommy."

Sadly, the awareness of the other children faded over time because of the power their parents gave to the Fear of the unknown. Marissa stayed connected to her ancestors in unseen yet tangible ways because Naomi taught her to remember.

As the girls grew, they began to develop other gifts. Marissa, who was a year younger than Lyndee, loved animals. She was always bringing home stray or wounded creatures. Animals of all kinds were drawn to her, and she seemed able to communicate with them on a level I had never seen before. It was not surprising to us when she began to work as a lab tech at the local veterinarian clinic, first on weekends then after school.

Once a large shepherd mix was brought to the clinic. The dog was so terrified that he refused to go back into the examining room. The kennel help finally called for

Marissa. She went to the front and spoke softly to the frightened animal. Then, with her hand resting on his head, he walked quietly beside her down the hallway to the examining room. That scenario was played over and over during her time there. It was a gift.

Animals were not the only ones who were drawn to Marissa. I went shopping with her one day, and though I did not particularly enjoy the activity myself, I looked for opportunities to spend time with her as I did with all three girls. A complete stranger came up to her on the sidewalk and began pouring out her problems to Marissa, who patiently listened and offered both comfort and advice.

I stood by, speechless, until the conversation ended then looked at Marissa, completely dumbfounded. "You realize that doesn't happen to everybody, don't you? I mean, complete strangers never come up to me and tell me their life stories!"

"It happens to me all the time," shrugged Marissa.

She and Lyndee both had the ability to communicate nonverbally, and they shared another gift as well. They could spot false teachings and lies from a mile away. Neither of them would let the issue pass, either. Especially Lyndee.

If Lyndee witnessed an injustice of any kind, she faced it head on. She did not hold back and she did not back down. If she knew she was right, she spoke up even when it was not politically correct to do so. Social conventions meant nothing to her. If a person was being unfair, it didn't matter who it was. She called them out. She was not afraid to say what everyone else was thinking, regardless of the cost to her.

One such incident involved her fourth grade teacher, Mrs. Briggs. Mrs. Briggs catered to certain students, mostly favoring those who came from what she considered to be "good" families. These children were, through no fault of their own, from prominent or influential families in the community.

Mrs. Briggs did something in class one day, and Lyndee responded by immediately raising her hand. "May I speak with you privately in the hall, please?" she asked politely.

When they reached the hallway, Lyndee explained bluntly (Lyndee was always blunt!), "You treat some people better than you do other people. You play favorites, and it isn't fair. You should treat everybody the same."

Mrs. Briggs denied that what she said was true, but the next day, Lyndee's hand went up again. "May I speak with you privately in the hall, please?"

When the door closed behind them once more, Lyndee tried again. "You see what you just did in there? That's exactly what I am talking about. You treat her better than you treat the rest of us."

Lyndee was right, and when she knew she was right, there was no stopping her. Righting wrongs seemed to be her mission in life. She battled injustice throughout her life, unafraid of the consequences.

As they grew, Naomi taught them to always trust their instincts. "You came here with those instincts, and you should always follow them." If either Marissa or Lyndee said someone gave them a "funny feeling," I learned to listen.

They watched after their younger sister Stephanie, caring for her and protecting her throughout her childhood. Marissa was always there to listen to her problems and offer wise counsel. Lyndee's role as her protector was a job she took very seriously. Just how seriously I discovered one afternoon after school when I found her sitting on top of a little boy, pounding his head on the ground in rhythm to the command, "Don't-you-ever-do-that-a-gain!" I learned that he had been trying to force his attentions on Stephanie. My guess is he never came near her again!

Stephanie, though not gifted in the same areas as her sisters, was nevertheless gifted in her own right. Coming to us seven years after Marissa was born, she received the full benefit of the understandings we had gained through maturity. I was an active part of her life agreement from her conception, and she entered this life knowing that she was loved before she made her agreement.

She was delicate, simple, and uncomplicated with a serenity that blanketed everyone and everything around her. She was a happy child and sang everywhere she went, making up songs about anything and everything. Her voice was so pure and sweet that everyone who heard her was captivated by the beauty of her tone. She began studying piano at an early age and seemed to enjoy the long hours of practice. Naomi particularly enjoyed her playing and would sit and listen to her practice for hours.

This life was truly a wonderful one. Our home was filled with music, laughter, and love. I was indeed a blessed man.

Chapter 17

I was pleased to see in my review that Naomi and I grew old together and that we were as much in love when she crossed over as we were the first time we laid eyes on one another. I saw the dozens of people that we helped understand that this life is only a layover in our earthly journey. "Enjoy every moment" was the message that we gave to others.

I was able to teach more than just language. I was able to share life and spread hope. Throw-away kids found a home with us, and Naomi took care of them all as though they were her own. She was the completion of me and showed me how selfless pure love was. Because of her support, I was able to lead a crusade to ease the suffering of children.

There is my grandson Jack. He is so beautiful. I am a little surprised that I will only meet him in passing. He and others of his generation will not forget, however, so he will remain open to communicating with me when I reach the other side.

He and those of his generation bring with them new gifts. They will usher in a time of universal love and understanding. They will arrive with the wisdom of the Knowing and will bring healing to the planet.

The final Knowing filled me with the power only known at the point of life and death, that critical point where we humans are one with the divine. This is the moment that we unconsciously seek throughout life. This feeling is the reason mind altering substances hold such fascination for humans. The euphoria known at this time brings perfect peace and comfort. Its closest approximation is attained only through deep Spirituality and meditation.

I was infused with comfort and felt the Knowing: *These are the days of prophecy fulfillment and revelation. All things will be known and seen by all of creation. The children are being born with the knowing that will not leave them as they grow old. Those who refuse to go forward will be left with nothing. There will be many who will stand alone in confusion looking for the answers they threw away.*
It is time now to move on to guide and help your children. Part of your agreement was that you will be the guiding ancestor for your descendants. You decided to stay as the soft still voice of knowing, unhindered by physical form.

I felt intense calm wash over me and carry me through the beautiful waves of Creation. True colors and waves of pure sound infused my senses and filled me with comfort. There were no more choices to make, only a promise to keep.

PART II

Marissa

GY Brown and PH Jones

Chapter 1

Where is Brad? If he wants to be here when this baby is born, he'd better get here soon!

For months my husband Brad and I had anticipated the birth of our first child. He was as involved in the pregnancy as any father could be. We attended birthing classes and spent hours picking out names. I wanted to keep the family tradition by passing on the names of my ancestors to my children. Brad had conceded even though passing on names in his family did not have the same meaning. He did like the idea of naming our son after my great grandfather, Thomas Jackson River.

My family's belief structure stemmed from Thomas's daughter, my grandmother Agnes. I relished the stories my mother and Aunt Sara told about her Native American heritage and how they applied those teachings to their lives. Agnes's great grandmother had survived the Long Walk and had organized the traditions so that they would not be lost. Her descendants were no longer recognized by the government, but they still held the genetic memory of the same Earthly truths.

My parents were an odd couple. My mother was one of the strongest women I knew. She could be firm –almost hard if her children were ever cruel or rude. My father was strong, too, and had a clear sense of my purpose so he never pushed me to be perfect or to fit into any one category. The school had talked my parents into letting me skip the 2nd grade. It was the one thing that my parents regretted about my childhood. The kids made fun of me because my father was a teacher and called me "Teacher's Pet" because I was more knowledgeable than the rest of them. I was never allowed to feel superior by my parents, however. They kept me grounded and held kindness as one of the greatest lessons they could teach us. Still I knew more than most because I came here with knowledge that I was encouraged to keep. I remembered long after many had forgotten.

My parents knew that I was smarter than my peers in many ways, but they felt I missed out on some important social development by not being with children my own age during those early years. The only good thing about that was that I was in the same grade as Lyndee after that.

Where is he? A lot of good those birthing classes were if my coach is not going to be here!!

As I lay in the delivery room, I tried to distract myself from the pain by thinking about my aunt Sara who was in the waiting room with Alex's little boys. It was no surprise that she had the little monsters again. Alex always had some reason for his mom to take care of them. Even at a time like this, he was as self absorbed as ever. My hope of having her at my side, saying just the right thing and coaxing me to see past the pain, was shattered like one of the lamps in the waiting room. I could hear it break even as far away as I was. I felt sorry for Aunt Sara because I knew that though she loved them dearly, she was longing to be with me to help bring my son into the world.

There was no end to the disrespect Alex gave his parents. Aunt Sara was my mother's sister, a renowned Medicine Woman who had been taught by their grandmother. My aunt never turned away anyone who was in need. Her healing gifts were legendary among indigenous Elders throughout the world. She was one of the few people who knew the old remedies and how to grow the herbs needed to make them. Yet I grew up watching great disrespect shown toward her on many occasions. As I grew old enough to understand what was happening, I would get angry and ask, "How can they do that? Don't they know who you are?" My aunt would say only that it was "part of the balance" and that it kept her humble. If I persisted she would repeat the stories I had heard a thousand times about how she had agreed to this life and all that came with it.

Aunt Sara and Uncle Henry had two boys, Billy and Alex. We heard stories about how jovial and happy Uncle Henry once was, always with a joke on the tip of his tongue. We knew that he was a highly decorated Marine. When he came back from Desert Storm, it was with a broken Spirit and body. He never talked about the war or his injury. We knew that he had an artificial leg, but we never knew what had happened. We could sense the affection people had for him and in turn we had a deep affection for him as well. Henry became the quiet observer of life.

Billy was a lot like his father. He was happy because he expected to find happiness. Growing up, Billy was the community hero, always championing the underdog. Bullies did not linger near Billy very long. Either they joined his group and embraced goodness, or they found another place to be. He adored his parents and little brother. Billy was determined every day to give his dad a reason to smile. His goal was to remove his father's hollow stare, which he saw often. When Alex came along he spoiled his little brother without shame and would only laugh when people would say it was not good for him. His reply was always the same, "Fruit spoils, not children".

Billy graduated from high school and promptly enlisted in the Marines. He thought it would make his father happy for him to follow in his footsteps. When the paperwork was already completed, he came home with a feast to celebrate. His parents were surprised when he appeared with fried chicken, cooked ham, deli salads, rolls and pies. There was much laughter and jabbing among Billy and the friends with whom he had enlisted. Aunt Sara did not join in the laughter but instead gave Billy a worried look.

After the meal Billy stood up and unfolded his enlistment papers. Uncle Henry took a deep breath when his eyes fell on the USMC seal. As Billy started reading, tears began to roll down Uncle Henry's cheeks. He left the table without a word. Aunt Sara dropped her head to hide her emotion, leaving Billy bewildered. He had thought that his parents would be overjoyed that he would be able to help with the finances.

Little Alex started to cry as their father left the room. He sensed that there was tension in his family, and he did not understand. Unhappiness filled his typically happy home. Billy had grown into a bear of a man but with one of the gentlest Spirits you would ever find. The horrors of war and life in the military would be a rude awakening for him. His parents knew that this was the last moment they would see their kind, happy son with peaceful innocence on his face. This was the last time they would hear that booming laugh that started low and grew to fill the house so that even the floorboards twisted in a smile.

A great Sadness entered their home that night. It went to work at once building a wall between Billy and his family. It was allowed to do this in order to begin building a buffer in Sara's and Henry's hearts for the time when the Sadness would claim its prize.

The day the chaplain knocked on the door, Aunt Sara invited him in and called Henry. Slowly they sat down to hear the news they already knew was coming. Billy was gone. Their boy was never coming home. A land mine in an unknown country in an unknown war had taken him.

After Billy was gone, Uncle Henry lost interest in everything, including Alex. As a result, Alex grew into a selfish young man. He was left to make his own choices, and usually those choices were not very good ones. Aunt Sara took the easy road and allowed Alex to have anything he wanted. She would pay a high price for her leniency.

Alex's cohort in crime and sometimes girlfriend was Evelyn, or Evie as she was called. Anytime Alex called from jail or woke up in a strange place, we knew that he was back with Evie. She appeared at Aunt Sara's house one day with a dirty baby in a dirty blanket. The poor child was screaming with hunger. She laid the baby on the tailgate of Uncle Henry's old truck, reached through the broken window, and honked the horn until Aunt Sara looked out. Then she just left.

Sara had no idea what to do with the abandoned child. She did not know where Alex was or if this was even his child. She took the baby in, cleaned and fed him, then started making phone calls. No one had seen Alex in months so she did not know where to begin to look. She was advised to care for the baby while the authorities tried to find Alex or Evie.

Alex was later found in a crack house across town and was taken to jail along with Evie. The two claimed that they had given their twins to Sara. This confession resulted in a frantic search for the second baby. The baby was found in a clothes hamper at a nearby laundromat. Evie and Alex were sent to prison for three years. Both were out within a year. At first it looked like they might have learned from their mistakes. They were clean and had jobs and a home. The state granted them custody of the two boys and all was well for a few months.

At some point Evie disappeared again. Alex continued to try to stay straight and maintain a stable home for the boys. It was clear that he was not any more of a parent then Evie was. He was in over his head and he knew it. There was no discipline, no regular diet, no routine, and little supervision of the boys. Mostly Alex would drop them off at Sara's and Henry's and would be gone for an unknown period of time to an unknown job that never paid. The boys were unmanageable. They could destroy a room in less than five minutes. Sara and Henry could not turn their backs for a second. We watched the life get sucked out of Aunt Sara. Most of us were afraid to say anything because we might be asked to help with the boys. We just watched with sadness and resentment toward Alex and his wild children.

I was brought back to the present by the sound of one of my sister Stephanie's compositions and realized it was the ring tone on my cell phone. Her music calmed me like it did everyone who heard her play. That gift was something I really needed right now! It was Brad's voice on the phone, and he sounded as desperate as a child lost in a crowd. "I'm almost there, Honey! This traffic is unreal!

There must be an accident up ahead, but I'll get there somehow. Hold on, Baby!"

Just then another pain hit me. All I could do was hold my breath and try not to make sounds that would distress him further. One gasp slipped out as I heard him shout, "Get out of my way! My wife's having a baby!!" As the contraction subsided, my mind wandered back to the first time I met Brad.

Bradley James Greeleaf. I remember thinking what a pompous name that was when I read the program schedule. We were at a weekend seminar on holistic medicine. He was there with a group of doctors for the purpose of debunking the healing practices they did not understand. As I spoke to the crowd about the benefits of therapeutic massage, he constantly interrupted me with irrelevant questions. He challenged me at every turn, finally claiming that no one who was not AMA certified could possibly know enough about the human body to heal it. He tried to say that the anatomy and physiology studied by massage therapists was a watered down version of what is required to truly understand the body. The debate became heated until finally I issued a challenge. I invited him to the stage to allow me to demonstrate my knowledge of the nervous system.

His friends urged him to take the challenge, and he reluctantly accepted. I began by identifying the pressure points used in acupressure and acupuncture. I demonstrated with each that I knew exactly where the nerves and controls were. Brad later told me that he
thought he was going to pass out. He wondered to this day how such a tiny hand could inflict so much pain and plea-

sure at the same time. I found every old injury. I identified every nerve and the muscle associated with it.

Later I told him it was his strength and resolve that attracted me to him that day, although I would never have admitted it at the time. By the end of the seminar, we realized that we shared a common goal - to heal people and remove pain and dysfunction.

A particularly hard contraction brought my mind back to the present, and I focused my attention on my breathing until it had passed.

Where can he be? I hope he is OK and that he isn't driving too fast.

I allowed my mind to wander again, back to how I got in this position in the first place. A few years after I had met Brad at the seminar, I applied for a job I had seen advertised at the local hospital. Medical facilities were finally recognizing the benefits of therapeutic massage, and I was eager to work there.

When I was called in for an interview, I was surprised to discover that Bradley Greeleaf was the doctor supervising the alternative program. Of course I was hired, and Brad told me it was that weekend years ago that had made him look at alternative medicine with an open mind. He had begun many programs that catapulted the hospital into the spotlight as a magnet hospital with an extraordinary reputation for diagnosing and healing difficult illnesses.

The chemistry between us was undeniable. I only worked there for a few months before we admitted that we would rather be a couple than employee and employer. So I went back into private practice and planned our wedding!

Chapter 2

We did not expect my father's death to bring on early labor. He had been slipping for a while and had taken great care to prepare us for his crossing. We knew that he wanted it to be a time of celebration rather than a time of grief since it would free him of the physical limitations that had plagued him for the last few years. His mind and Spirit would be free to explore the universe like a child skipping through the park in the spring. And he would be with Mom. Before his crossing he often forgot she was gone and frequently looked for her.

We understood that the physical body was designed to cling to life, having the basic survival instinct programmed at conception. The will to live is the strongest of all involuntary instincts. It allows the mind and Spirit the freedom to experience life without having to constantly be reminded to breathe, move, blink, etc. As one's life force grows weaker in the physical body, it grows stronger in the Mental and Spiritual body. The closer we are to the Creative force with whom we are one, the less we need a body.

The death struggle takes on many forms and can appear to be a fight for life at times during the transition from the physical experience back to the Spiritual existence. Usually the physical struggle is greater when loved ones attempt to keep people here past their appointed time. The reason can be anything from fear of life without them to regrets of various kinds.

This is just like Dad! It is so like him to distract us right now!

Dad had always been good at creating distractions when life was getting tough or just too serious. I recalled how Mom would smile when he would start calling with silly made up problems at stressful times. He had a way of always knowing when to play the clown. When we would come home from school feeling bad because of the cruelty of other children, he would jump from behind a curtain or door with a funny face and make us laugh. We couldn't help ourselves. We would forget the slight and hurt just long enough for us to get it into perspective.

It was clear that he wasn't going to allow any sadness now, either. I wished that he could have held on long enough to know his grandson. I wished I could have comprehended his words when he explained that he would be with us like his mother was with him. I never told him that I did not understand what he meant. He was so sure and credited his normalcy to his mother's presence in his life even though she had died in childbirth.

I really hope my son waits for his father to get here before making his grand entry! We have both worked so hard to make his birth a good experience.

The midwife was saying, "It is almost time, Mrs. Greeleaf. You are one centimeter away. Where did your husband say he was?" I could not even answer her as another pain ripped through my body.

What was I thinking when I insisted on doing this naturally? Giving birth like my ancestors seemed like such a good idea at the time.

The room filled with hospital personnel bringing in medical equipment. "It's time!" said the midwife as she smiled. "I don't think he is going to wait for his daddy. Breathe, slow down, push, relax, breathe".

I felt the door open and looked over to see a nurse trying to put a gown on Brad and get him scrubbed in.

"I'm here, I'm here, Honey!" Brad called out as he rushed to my side. I grabbed his arm and gasped, "I can't do this! It hurts too much!"

I heard him say, "Sure you can! Now push - hard!" I felt a sudden burning release as my son's head crowned. Brad's soothing voice encouraged me to breathe, push, rest. All I could hear was my heart pounding. Then our son was laid on my stomach while they did what was necessary to secure his disconnect from me. Bradley Jackson Greeleaf appeared to turn his head and look around the room blinking. The old ones that had birthed many babies were not surprised.

The babies being born into the world these days from healthy mothers arrived awake and knowing. Those who did not were born of parents who either abused drugs or alcohol or passed on some genetic weakness. Some of these young ones would never recover and would carry issues forward throughout the rest of their lives, making the rest of society obligated to care for them. Luckily in this country that is what happens. In much of the world that is not what happens. Many are put to death as soon as

the problems manifest themselves. Some are put to death merely because they are a female. It is hard to understand that in this time of enlightenment such things were still happening.

Jack. You are so beautiful. Your perfection at this moment is breathtaking.

I always wondered why people would say a wrinkly, red faced newborn was beautiful. I would look at the photographs thinking that there was little to call beautiful, and I hoped for the parents' sake that something changed so as to make the child more physically attractive. Now, though, I understood. The beauty they come with is not physical. It is an eternal beauty representing the ongoing life through Creation. It is the beauty of a promise kept between mankind and the Creator. It is the confirmation of the divinity of life. Yes, wrinkles and red blotches are beautiful.

Brad and I were alone in a room full of people. We realized that our life agreement had changed forever and that we were responsible for a life other than our own. I realized that it was up to Jack now to confirm his life agreement. I desperately hoped that he would find in us everything he needed to become the person he was meant to be. I vaguely thought that I should feel empty after his birth but I didn't. It was as though my maternal instincts swelled to fill the void where Jack had been developing for the last eight and a half months. There was no emptiness, only unconditional love and wonder. I was so very thankful to feel the instincts grow and the knowledge pour in. I had heard from some women that they did not experience an awakening of ancestral knowledge with the birth of their first child. It would be very frightening not to instinctively know what to do. I supposed that was the reason parenting books were always on the best seller list. I thought perhaps I should keep a journal and write one in a few years.

Jack was returned to us after a brief check-up in another room. As we gazed into one another's eyes, I felt the unmistakable presence of my father.

"He is beautiful, Sweetheart. I am so proud of you! And I want you to know that I will always be near watching over him – and you."

I smiled through my tears and knew everything was as it should be. I felt warm and happy and complete.

This perfect moment was over soon, however, when a nurse asked if we were ready for the rest of the family to come in. As much as I would have liked to have held onto this moment forever, I knew that I had to allow Brad's parents to see their first grandchild. My mother-in-law Gloria was a spoiled woman, very much accustomed to having her way. She was brought up to feel superior as a privileged southern belle. She still talked about her debutant ball as though it happened just last week. She even had the dried yellow roses to prove how spectacular it was and brought them out with little encouragement.

At first she was unbearable because in her limited view Brad had married beneath himself. Time softened her attitude toward me as she saw how much we loved each other. She realized that I was not after the family money or the name that she so valued. She had actually been very loving throughout my pregnancy and was a big help in preparing the nursery. She even surprised me with an in-depth thought or two once in a while. She did love her children and her husband, I admitted early in our relationship. Now I sensed that her love extended to me through the birth of her grandchild. Maybe there was hope for us to be close one day.

Chapter 3

Jack was a wonder. Although I was exhausted from the birthing, I could not look away from him. I was afraid that if I took my eyes off him for a moment, the whole experience might dim. I wanted every single second of this remarkable event to be etched into my mind forever.

The tenderness that I saw in my husband added a new facet to him which I had not seen before. Brad had always been kind and loving, but when he held Jack there was a new softness on his face and a glow in his eyes. The career driven man I knew so well was tempered with the marvel of creation.

When it was time to leave the hospital, a nurse appeared with a wheelchair to take us to the loading area. Brad went to get the car while I waited, holding our precious child. As I looked around me, I noticed other women waiting with their babies, too. There were stark differences, it is true, but the fact that we were all life givers made us all related not just as a species but as guardians of the future generation.

I looked at my fellow new mothers, eager to share a thought or a smile about our new status as life givers. With a shock, I realized that many of them were distracted, almost aloof as they waited. Some did not even look happy and seemed to be disdainful of their situation. I was taken aback and waited in silence while I watched the others get picked up one by one.

I watched as an old woman drove up and got out to help what must have been her daughter into an old sedan. I noticed the new mother wore several pairs of old, thin socks on this cold day but that the new baby wore only what the hospital provided. It made me sad to think that this young mother might be going home to a life of need. It was clear that they were without many of life's basics and that another mouth to feed was a great concern.

The next woman to be picked up looked thin and unhealthy. Her baby was crying loudly as she tried in vain to comfort it. A young man in a loud smoking truck drove up to get them. It took a while for the hospital staff to help him strap in a car seat. I watched as he worked to secure a trash bag which had been placed over a window opening. In his excitement he kept taping the bag to himself instead of the window.

When the young man was satisfied that his smoky chariot was ready for his little family, he reached down and lifted the slim new mother into the truck. He placed her in the seat with such tenderness that it brought tears to my eyes. When he had made her comfortable, he ran around to the other side of the truck where, under the watchful eyes of the hospital staff, he placed the baby ever so gently in its car seat, facing backwards in the middle of the raggedy bench seat. The baby had stopped crying and was almost asleep before the young man finished tucking the blankets around his treasured family.

The next new mother was impatiently waiting with a bevy of well dressed relatives. Her constant sighs and disgusted gasps were embarrassing to her family. The nurse waiting with her turned to another nurse, and they exchanged a look that said, "I am so glad she is leaving!" When her ride appeared, she promptly declared that she was not going to go home in that vehicle and demanded that one of the older men in the group bring the better automobile around. The staff loaded her flowers and balloons into the car she had rejected while they waited for the older man to bring the approved one for this obviously spoiled woman and her child.

Finally I spotted Brad's smiling face behind the wheel of our rather average-looking minivan. His exuberance filled the space with excitement as he strained forward, willing the other vehicles to hurry. Once he had placed us safely in the car and we were on our way home, I settled into the seat comfortably and began to doze.

In semi-consciousness I marveled at the fact that all babies are born with the same promise and potential. They all come with very few expectations of others. They have agreed to come into these tiny bodies to experience life as humans. Watching the vastly different mothers of those other infants was eye opening and troubling for me. I had seen many animal babies come into the world at the veterinary clinic where I worked when I was in high school. There a dog was a dog no matter what breed, a cat was a cat, and so on.

Healthy human babies all start out the same, too, but they are put out on different playing fields even as they leave the hospital. All the shouting about equality in our county had no bearing on the reality of what I had just witnessed in that pick up line. I hoped that one of the new gifts of this generation would lead us to true equality without judgment. All babies deserve that. I wondered how much their environment influenced their choice to stay. I quickly discounted that thought remembering that miscarriage, sudden infant death, and other infant casualties crossed all lines of humanity. The only thing that seemed different was the judgment of others. If a family was poor, they were under more scrutiny than someone who was affluent. Perhaps that too will change in this generation.

I wonder how many people come to Earth full of hope, bringing with them a new awareness, only to be ignored, discounted, or even erased because of some minor difference? Will the baby who left in the smoking truck have a great gift for healing? Will she be ignored because her parents are poor? Will the child without a father present be ridiculed for it until he is beaten down and left with no self esteem? I sure hope that Jack and his peers are kinder than my generation and those before have been. After all, they are all born with the same hope.

In parts of the world where the number of children was limited, parents would not risk having a child that was less than perfect. If there were a physical flaw, it could mean the end to the parents' descendents. This seemed to me a good example of too much government.

Maybe that is why so many differences are not detected until later in life. It protects the messenger until they are loved enough to be of value in this society.

My wandering thoughts had always been considered a little odd by those who did not see the bigger picture as I did.

How long will it be before the government here controls the birth of children? They already control the medications they can be given - what chemicals can enter their tiny bodies. They use Fear to control parents and make them feel that they are not good parents if they question the system that injects foreign chemicals into their little ones in the name of protection. They create labels to place on children who are the least bit different, then recommend therapies and medications to alter their behavior so that they conform. Parents are attacked for defying these protocols. Parents who fight for their children's right to be themselves – to be different - are viewed as odd or uncooperative. When did 'unique' become 'different?'

So many times my father and I had talked about the fact that the future was not for the poor or sick. They were the groups most likely to become test subjects for medications for the wealthy. If one of the medicines happened to work, then the wealthy would then make it out of reach for the poor. The failure of the health care system, my father said, started with the human who directed what could be used, who could see what doctors, and so forth.

"It happened slowly, over time," Dad said. "It came in looking like something great that was going to help lots of people. People accepted it, and it took control of everything. It made my father sad that most people could not see what was really happening.

I smiled as I felt him stroke my hair now. "Jack's generation holds the promise of all things good and equal. The disappearance of economic lines starts here. Recognizing the gifts of all children and the value of each and every one begins now. Labels and experimental treatments will vanish. The future will be better with understanding and respect for life as a sacred choice. Each person will be recognized as having an individual life agreement, and each will be given the respect to live that life."

I felt content and realized that we were almost home. In more ways than one.

GY Brown and PH Jones

Chapter 4

My peaceful dozing ended as we turned into our neighborhood. "Welcome home, Jack" banners and blue bows were everywhere. Our cul-de-sac was aflutter with blue and white ribbons, making me recall a Taffy Pull we once had when I was twelve.

I could hear Dad's laughter as clearly as though he were right there. Somewhere he got the idea that a Taffy Pull would be a good way to celebrate Halloween. Mom never allowed us to celebrate it because she said we were not going to give our good energy to the other side by pretending all that ghoulishness was a good thing. "I will get you candy because I love you, not because someone declares that we should honor the unseen of their world."

How he convinced her that a Taffy Pull was a good idea, I will never know. We wondered about that at the time, too, but Dad always knew how to get around Mom if we wanted something. He got all the ingredients together and she made the candy base. The color they used was blue, and we had all my friends over. My sisters were as excited as I was. We were so glad we were finally able to celebrate the strange holiday like normal people! Before the evening was over there were bits of sticky candy everywhere. We found blobs of it in the most unlikely places for months. Mom was not happy, but every time Dad found one of the sticky memories, his eyes would twinkle.

I was brought back to the present when the door to the minivan opened. Brad's mother barely restrained a squeal of happiness as she reached in to unfasten the car seat. "Wait a minute, Gloria!" I cried. The alarm in my voice caused everyone to pause. I was fumbling to unfasten my seatbelt and move with as little pain as possible when I realized everyone was staring at me. Brad broke the silence by proudly declaring what a protective new mother I was. "She is already the mother bear," he said proudly. The moment lightened, but I could see the hurt on Gloria's face. For all her pettiness, she really had a good heart. I hugged her and thanked her for being there to help and to welcome us home. She helped me inside while Brad brought our precious son into our home for the first time. I would have liked for it to have been just the three of us, but I realized that was a selfish thought and that Jack had agreed to be here because of all the people who would love him.

Glitter? Lots of glitter! I will never get it out of everything! What is the woman's fascination with glitter? She is so elegant and has such good taste in everything else. What is the deal with the glitter?

My resistance was down, making it hard to mask my displeasure at the puffs of glitter everywhere. Gloria saw my concern but misunderstood the thin smile on my face.
She gushed, "I am so glad you love glitter, too! My family would never allow anything like that in the house, and I love it so much. It reminds me of Angel Kisses!" The tight smile on my face relaxed. I looked at my mother-in-law as if I was seeing her for the first time.

Bless her heart. There is such a frail woman under that hard exterior.

From that moment on, I never saw glitter again. I saw instead Gloria's Angel Kisses.

I was too exhausted to enjoy the welcome home feast and asked the others to enjoy the food while Jack and I took a nap. Brad took us upstairs to rest. I could not put my baby in his bed right away and laid him in our bed with me. We fell asleep right away with Brad watching over us and our loved ones laughing downstairs. "What a beautiful moment," I thought as I drifted off in a contented sleep.

Oh, wow! This baby has a set a lungs!

I woke to the screaming demand for food from our indignant little one. The glump-glump noise was Brad bounding up the stairs to see what all the screaming was about. He came to a screeching halt in the doorway when he saw that I was sitting up in our bed feeding our son. He came over and gently knelt beside the bed, his eyes wet with tears of happiness. "Can I do anything for either of you?" I shook my head and smiled. He kissed us both and went back downstairs.

What a wonderful start this is to your life, sweet one! Surely you know how much you are loved! Your life agreement will be easily filled here with us. All those people downstairs came to welcome you home. They love you and will be in your life as long as you want them to be.

He woke every hour through the night. He was having a hard time adjusting to home life and seemed to have his days and nights mixed up. It took a few days for us to establish a routine, but once we did life became much easier. Gloria stayed with us during the day while Brad was at work. My friends brought over supper for a few days, and we would eat together.

After the first week I was strong enough to take care of things myself. I convinced Gloria that there was no need for her to come every day. She protested, but the dark circles and slow movements told me she was exhausted and needed rest, too. I reassured her that she was always welcome and would be able to enjoy her grandson more after she had rested. Her smile at my concern for her was genuine.

My mother instilled in me many basic Native American values. One was being thankful for each day and honoring it. To wake without being thankful was unheard of in our home. There were many things about Mom that others did not understand. It didn't matter to her what others thought when it came to honoring the Ancestors. She burned the herbs of honor and cleansed our surroundings faithfully. "Every day is Sacred," she would say. "We don't limit our thankfulness to one or two days a week. It is every single day, every little moment."

I was beginning to see as a new mother that this lesson was not as easy as it sounded. It was hard to focus on much of anything in the mornings when the baby was crying and Brad was hurrying to get ready for work. I wondered how Mom did it with three children. She had a garden full of work waiting for her, and she made sure there was good food for us to eat. So far I had not figured out how to prepare meals from scratch like she did and take care of a baby, too. Maybe that was something I would learn in time.

I found that I was much more emotional than I had been before Jack was born. I wondered if this was normal and hoped that I was not developing one of the new mother syndromes. I expressed this concern to Brad one night while eating supper. He looked at me with wide eyes at first then his face eased into a smile. He hugged me and reassured me that I was normal and that the increased emotions were the result of hormonal changes. The changes were good, he said, and supported motherhood by increasing my maternal awareness.

My frown turned into a chuckle then as I thought about Brad's telling me about awareness of anything. He had come a long way since that weekend years ago when he heckled me from the audience. "Do you realize how aware you have become over the last few years?" I asked.

He gazed out the window for a moment before answering. "I think it just came naturally and slowly. There is no denying the power of the unseen or the instincts of all living things. Survival of a species is the evidence that supports instinct. Surely Neanderthal man had acute awarenesses to survive and evolve into higher thinkers. Otherwise he would not have survived at all and would have been devoured by wild animals in his sleep. Something had to be whispering in his ear telling him to wake up or die. I myself have felt that tingling sensation on the back of my neck that said, 'Listen up, something is different!'"

I wondered for moment about the scientists who insist that reality is only what you see.

How do they convince themselves that nothing exists without physical proof? I wonder how they will feel when they discover that their life agreements included chasing a theory that was so utterly false. How will they balance all the time and energy spent convincing people that there is no unseen? They will probably have to come back here as either theologians or visionaries.

I looked down at my sweet Jack, now sleeping peacefully, and felt the presence of the Ancestors all around us.

Chapter 5

Life with Jack is such exhausting fun! I am so thankful he chose us as his parents! I love the way he breaks into that baby giggle which comes from within his Spirit. It engulfs everything and everyone in its pure infectious happiness. No one can hear that sound without smiling. Even on the worst day the sound of a baby giggling makes everything better.

His first steps were such an accomplishment to Brad and me. We were so excited that we took all sorts of pictures while we exclaimed how wonderful he was. Jack just gave us a look which said, "What are you so excited about? This is nothing."

It was no surprise when the phone rang shortly after he took his first steps. It always seemed that Jack communicated with other family members, especially when he crossed what we considered to be a milestone. It was my sister Stephanie. I started to tell her the exciting news, but she was already asking me how far he had walked before I could get the words out.

How do you do that? How do you know what is happening in my house before I tell you?

I was a little disappointed that I was not able to share the news with Steph. Truth to tell, though, she was not the only one who could pick up on what I was thinking. Lyndee and Aunt Sara always knew, too. They constantly strengthened my belief in universal synchronicity by trusting the messages they got and acting on them.

A couple weeks before Jack took his first steps, we had an early cold spell. I turned on the heat and only cold air came out. I was frantically looking for a repair company when the door bell rang. There stood Aunt Sara with an electric blanket and a beautiful quilt! A few moments later Lyndee arrived with an electric space heater she had picked up at a yard sale on her way over. It was comforting to know that we shared the ability to communicate without words.

As I walked with them to their cars, I saw a panel van moving slowly through our subdivision. On the side was painted <u>HAVAC Cooling and Heating</u>! I waved them down and told them to come in, thinking that Brad must have called them. After they repaired the heating unit, I noticed the name on the paperwork: Cheschozky. When I told them that was the wrong paperwork, the man seemed puzzled. "Isn't this the Cheschozky residence?" I said no. Several moments of awkward silence followed as we looked at each other trying to figure out what had just happened. He muttered something in what sounded like Italian, gave me the paperwork, got paid and left whistling a pleasant tune.

That evening I told Brad about the incident. He was so tired from a long shift at the hospital that he was already dozing off. He muttered, "Your dad sent them, didn't he?" He opened his eyes then with a slight frown, wondering what he had just said. I smiled and kissed him goodnight, a little disappointed that I hadn't thought of that already.

Maybe it *was* Dad who had sent the repairmen. Maybe it was the Knowing. Maybe we were all tuning in to the same world at the same time so that we knew the needs of those around us. Mom always said there would come a time when the spoken word would not be needed. She believed that everyone would be able to hear thoughts and act on them. She also said that we would need less and less in the way of material things and sustenance to be whole and happy. She spoke of these things with such confidence that I believed it even though I did not understand it.

She taught us to live our lives as if the whole world were watching because there would come a time when it would become true. She said that one day there would be no hidden intentions, good or bad. I felt that I had only halfway listened to her most of the time, but now I realized that I had heard her clearly. Not only had I heard her clearly, I had internalized the understandings.

Jack's first steps were followed by his first words. Only his words were not clear to everyone. He communicated well with us and seemingly with other children - but not with adults outside our family. I discovered this as I planned to go back to work and was looking for day care. Each of the three interviews concluded with the day care director asking me for Jack's diagnosis. I was taken aback and was more than a little agitated at such a ridiculous question. Then I started to worry that something was really wrong.

I asked Brad to find a doctor who might be able to test him to discover if there was a problem. Brad felt that he was a little slow to talk, as some boys are, and that he was perfectly normal. I, being a new mother and somewhat anxious, insisted that he set up the appointment so he arranged everything through one of his colleagues.

We took Jack to see Dr. Brawn, whom Brad had met in medical school. After a couple of hours of testing I was ushered into Dr. Brawn's office and asked to wait. The nurse told me they had paged Brad and that he would be there shortly. Waiting was hard - my heart was racing and my head began to hurt. Jack was sound asleep in my arms without a worry in the world. I should have taken my cue from the sleeping smiles on his face that there was nothing to worry about. Like all new mothers I was afraid there might be something wrong, and I wanted to be sure. The nurse popped back in to ask if he could get me anything. I shook my head and tried to smile.

That's not a good sign! He's trying to put me at ease. That must mean that there is something coming that is going to make me uneasy! Where are you, Brad?

Finally I could hear him and Dr. Brawn talking in hushed tones just outside the door. I felt a sense of dread as they entered the room. I could not read Brad's face and followed his gaze to Dr. Brawn's face. He began to speak in a calm voice that was full of sympathy. "Marissa, I am sorry to tell you that, based on preliminary tests, I think Jack might have mild Autism. " I felt the color drain from my face.

Mild Autism? What do you mean mild Autism?

I barely heard the rest of the explanation and all the results that led him to this impossible conclusion. He was saying something about more tests and possible therapies, but I didn't hear very much else.

We left the office in silence. My mind cried out for Aunt Sara just as my cell phone rang. It was Aunt Sara telling me that she was on her way over. She asked if I needed her to bring anything but all I could do was burst into tears. The short ride home seemed to take forever. The lump in my throat was choking me, and I couldn't breathe. Finally we turned onto our street.

I saw Aunt Sara's car as we topped the hill. She was at the van even before it stopped. She opened the door and embraced me, supplying the comfort I needed so badly. She stroked my hair as I sobbed, telling me everything would be alright. Slowly I composed myself and got out of the van. Brad stood helplessly by as we gathered our peacefully sleeping Jack out of the car seat and went inside. Feeling sympathy for Brad in his empty handed awkwardness, Aunt Sara suggested that he put Jack upstairs to finish his nap. His relief at having something useful to do was evident.

Sara continued to take care of everything, gently ordering me to sit on the sofa while she brewed some tea. I was numb. When she came back into the living room with the warm tea, I realized that I was still wearing my coat. She set the teapot on the coffee table and took my coat. When we were settled with our tea she asked me to tell her what had happened.

Chapter 6

After a few sips of Chamomile tea, Aunt Sara told me to start from the beginning. I didn't need any more encouragement and burst out tearfully, "Jack has autism!"

Aunt Sara laid her hand gently on my arm and looked at me with a solid stare. I felt the tension start to relax in my jaw and slowly filter down through the rest of my body. It was only then that I realized how much tension and stress I had been carrying. My jaw hurt as I released my clenched teeth, and I started to tremble. My arm began to regain its feeling as the warmth of Aunt Sara's touch thawed me from the inside out.

Sanity slowly returned, and I started back at the beginning. This all started, I told her, because I wanted to return to work a couple of days a week. It was important to me not to lose any of the certifications I had worked so hard to earn. Plus, the extra money would help cover the medical expenses from Jack's birth. I began looking for daycare centers and made appointments for Jack and me to visit several of them. At first I had not understood the way in which the workers would motion each other to the side or turn their backs to me while they discussed the possibility of Jack's coming to their facility. The first center told me that they could put him on a waiting list. The second told me that they would schedule him for an evaluation. I went away wondering why they would need to evaluate him, and the next day I called to ask why.

After being put on hold for a very long time, I was told that they needed to see what kind of "interpretive care" he would require. I still did not understand. But when I went to the third center, I told them there was no need for evaluations or tests. The director asked what diagnosis he had already been given. I was confused. "Diagnosis for what?" I demanded. The man became oddly frustrated, reached into his desk, and handed me a business card where he said I could get some answers.

Aunt Sara was sitting back in her chair now with a much more relaxed look on her face. Her demeanor steadied me, and I began to feel as if I were reciting a scene from a play. I explained the interviews and testing that followed at the child development center. They observed his interactions with other children and with adults. Sara asked at once who did the observations and tests. When I told her the staff and teachers did the screening, she set down her tea and held both of my hands in hers.

"A long time ago we were allowed and encouraged to be one with all in the universe. We understood the animals, the trees, and all other living things. We knew the names of all the stars and welcomed them as they passed overhead at different times of the year. We lived with the seasons and ate the food of those seasons. We were healthy most of the time. If we had an illness, the medicine to cure it was within an arm's reach. Our intuitions were sharp and there was no need for very many words. Our communication was unspoken. As people who had always been here on this Continent there were no unknowns. We just knew that we knew.

Later other people came from other places. They talked differently, had different beliefs, ate different foods, and brought with them illnesses we did not understand.

They saw us as healthy and carefree. Some of them had never seen such carefree humans before and thought that we might have been deranged. They had mental illnesses where they came from and had made a habit of identifying behavior they did not understand as mental illness. Soon after they came, we began to have illnesses that we did not understand. We did not know that it was the germs and ill intentions of these newcomers that were making us sick. Some went to our medicine people for help. The new people did help some of our people heal from the diseases that they brought. This gave them power because of the reverence we gave healers. In the confusion we did not see that these people could not hear with thought-words or feel what another feels. They could not sense pain in another or see when someone was sad. They could not hear the trees cry when they were cut or burned. By the time we realized that these new people were deaf to the unspoken, it was too late.

    This has continued since that time. In the 1950's their governing agents and their doctors sent teams to our reservation homes to try to discover why we could still hear the unspoken. Many of our children were damaged in the process of their investigations. But some were able to carry on and fight to make a place for truth to be heard.

    In the 1960's, children from all people began being born with the old gifts of hearing the unspoken, seeing the unseen, and deciphering the truth. They had to fight to clear the paths for the army of seers that were coming. The children from this time were called trouble makers, pot heads, hippies and other names in an effort to degrade and isolate them. These children went on to become part of the system that was wrong in an effort to change it. Sadly they have been outnumbered greatly. It is the gentle strength they posses along with the eternal knowledge that life does not begin and end here that powers them on still.

The number of aware people continued to grow. In the 1970s there were many more, and they began to find each other. One way they found each other was when schools started labeling them. We saw the people in authority become frightened. In their Fear they developed drugs to change what they were seeing in aware people. They gave them labels like hyperactive, dyslexic, and so on. They developed procedures to keep the number of aware people from growing and made many of them dependent on drugs and government handouts. They took away their power and with it their ability to hear and see the unseen.

Some survived, but the numbers were greatly depleted. The few who did survive had an even greater struggle in overcoming the labels. Only the strongest were able to learn code shifting to escape the labels and drugs. The very strongest warriors of intuition among them have had to retreat into silence. Nevertheless, they have stood firm, helping quietly whenever possible. They have had an uphill battle finding camaraderie in their differences.

The decade of the 1980s brought more labels since the number of aware children was once again growing. The schools became tools of oppression and separation. They increased funding for specialized programs, broadened their scope, and divided children according to contrived standards that created specific categories of "disabilities." Tests were designed and geared to effectively place certain knowings in controlled environments designed to suppress natural growth. "Gifted" took on a whole new meaning. The "gifted" had to meet a narrow and specific set of academic standards. Membership to this group was the goal of most. Few who followed their inner voice could be included in this group. It was that way by design. Those labeled "gifted" were soldiers of convention not awareness. Those who had life agreements that involved unconventional challenges were labeled as "special needs." A label was created for those who were too intelligent to be isolated, too. They were called "behavior disordered." They had a cage for everyone who was aware.

Still they kept coming. In the 1990's more categories had to be generated to control the new wave of children. ADD and ADHD came into the picture along with the drugs to control them. The arsenal to shoot down anything different kept growing, and the weapons to stifle the awareness got stronger and stronger.

Here we are in the 2000s. Is it any surprise that there are more disorders, more therapies, more drugs, more "problems" to control? The numbers of the newly gifted are growing exponentially. This wave of aware children seems unstoppable. Those who have Fear of things they do not understand are desperately working to control the flood of Knowing.

We are coming full circle now. We are back to having the choice to give the power back to the Knowing or to the Fear.

You know that our Prophecies clearly tell us that this circle will come back around to the Knowing. We know that there will be children from all backgrounds who will join the circle of Knowing. They will come from all walks of life and every corner of the Earth. We know that there will not be any separation based on skin color, beliefs, economics, or age.

My dear Marissa, before you forget what you know, who you are, and what your life agreement is - stop and consider these things. Jack came to you because of what he saw in you - not what he saw in others. You need to fulfill his vision by acting on what you know, what you remember. Do not take on the Fear of others as your own. If something was truly wrong with him, you would have known it before hearing what another person thought."

I felt so peaceful. The words my wise Aunt spoke resonated in my Spirit as truth. It made so much sense and was so simple. We each had our agreement and our mission. We were the authors of our own stories - stories that were already written. We were the wisdom of all our Ancestors. The calm voice of understanding penetrated my soul and transformed the Fear to strength.

I could see that there would be many struggles in order for my son to continue hearing the voice within him. The thought that I would have to stand out and be different filled me with trepidation.

Aunt Sara saw this and addressed it at once. "You are strong enough to withstand anything that comes your way as you champion those who are too young to speak for themselves. You are the one who will bring light to the darkness created by Fear. You will turn the mirror on oppression, forcing it to look at itself. You will move the innocent out of the way when Fear pushes so that it has nothing to push against but itself. You have been granted a great opportunity to protect and nurture one who still hears. Do not cringe in fear of falsehoods designed to oppress truth!"

As Aunt Sara delivered her final speech, I felt my spine straighten and my eyes open. Everything looked brighter. My senses were coming alive. Oddly, then, I realized I was starving! When I told Sara that I was hungry, she laughed and went to her car. She was back in a moment carrying the meal she had made for us - her famous potato salad, fried chicken, sweet tea, and coconut pound cake.

That was the thing about my mother's sister. She thought of everything!

GY Brown and PH Jones

Chapter 7

I don't know how parents with more than one child keep up! I don't remember having homework in first grade. I don't remember Mom having such a hard time keeping up with the housework, meals and getting us where we needed to be on time. She had three of us to take care of and did better than I am doing with one!

I knew Brad was doing all he could to help me at home when he was there and awake. I really thought his seniority would keep him from being the one to take up the slack from budget cuts at work. He seemed, however, to be keeping his job by doing the work of three doctors.

My neighbor was always making comments about how we were so lucky because Brad was a doctor. The neighbor assumed that sick people kept us in high end cars and jewelry. She made me really angry one day when she saw me drive up and came to ask where my new car was. When I looked at her in confusion she continued, "I just got the bill for my emergency room visit last month. I figured you would have already bought a new car."

If she only knew! The days when doctors made lots of money in an over-priced system were gone. Some months I had made more money than Brad! The economy had crushed so many people that many of them had no insurance. Brad treated them anyway. There was also the high cost of malpractice insurance. People were so anxious to sue that no doctor in his right mind would practice without it. If we were in medicine for the money, we would be doing something different, somewhere else. I just remarked on the weather, as my mom taught me, and left her standing there in her bitterness.

As I turned to Jack to take off his coat, I realized that he was still gazing at the neighbor. He was standing at the window looking toward her house. I wondered what he could possibly be thinking and called out his name. He slowly turned toward me with a distant smile as if he were somewhere else. I wondered what made my baby look off into the distance so often. What was he seeing? More importantly what was he doing?

I had seen that same look many times before on my mother's face when she was "working on something." It occurred to me that maybe they were "working on" my neighbor together. I could hope for that, anyway!

"Time for a nap, little boy" I told him. He rubbed his eyes with his little fists as if the mention of a nap reminded him that he was tired. I was sure that other moms would be critical of the way we got our sleep. We would come in and take a little nap in the afternoon so that Jack could stay up later to see his dad. This time together was important for both of them, and as long as Jack was getting the rest he needed, I didn't think it mattered when or how he was getting it.

Jack did so love to keep a routine. I took his hand and started upstairs. As I tucked him in, I thought I caught a whiff of my mother's herbs which made me smile. I felt an overwhelming urge to join Jack in a nap. As if he sensed this in me, he patted the place next to him in his new big boy bed. It did not take any more convincing. I gratefully curled up with him and drifted off to sleep.

The dream started as nothing out of the ordinary. I saw my life now as I went about my day. I was standing in the kitchen, still in my oversized sleep shirt. I could tell that I needed to hurry to get the day started, but I lingered with the cup of coffee a little longer than usual. Jack looked at me and smiled over his bowl of cereal. I heard the shower upstairs as Brad started his day. I smiled and heard my dad whistling his morning tune. As I turned, I realized that the bacon I smelled was cooked by my mom. I could almost taste the smoky fat. Even in my dream I wondered how all of this could be possible.

This is weird. I am in the present, but my past is superimposed on it. The strangest part is that it seems perfectly normal. But I know I am in a deep sleep!

I started to wake and opened my eyes to see Jack sound asleep beside me. I wondered at the dream but realized with a start that I could still smell bacon! I don't cook bacon, and there had never been any in my home. Moving slowly so as to not disturb Jack, I slid off the bed and tiptoed downstairs. No bacon, no Mom or Dad, no shower running - nothing. I shook my head in bewilderment and started to work on supper.

Soon Jack awoke and came downstairs, dragging his book bag excitedly into the kitchen. He climbed up into the chair, book bag still in tow, and with great enthusiasm began getting out his "work." I asked, "What do you have, there, Buddy?" He seemed not to hear me as he started placing his art work at the place next to him at the table. He leaned over and pointed to various things on the paper while talking in a language I did not understand. His words were few but his exclamations of joy went on and on. After a bit of pointing and explaining, he sat back with his feet under him in the chair. He hugged his arms to him while scrunching up his shoulders and laughed as if to say, "I am happy they like it." He leaned over to collect his art work and said he was going to put it up so that everyone could see it. Running to the refrigerator, he posted his masterpiece there with oversized magnets. As he backed away to admire the placement, he looked past me to the table and nodded.

I held my breath for fear of disturbing them. I knew that he was talking to our Ancestors and sharing his day with them. He climbed back up in the chair, pulling his reader out of his bag. "Mamma, I am reading now," he said in his clear, little boy voice. There was a trace of a shared secret in his smile. I smiled, too, and marveled at how naturally my baby could visit with those who had gone to the place I couldn't always see.

Ground turkey helper was on the menu that night. As I rummaged through the refrigerator, Jack slid in front of me and started rummaging, too. I stepped back to give him some room. He pulled out a pack of precooked turkey bacon, turned, and handed it to me, asking if we could have it for supper. I told him that we were having ground turkey in a casserole. Again he looked past me and nodded, putting the turkey bacon back in the refrigerator and skipping back to his chair.

"Better get your homework finished before Daddy comes home so you can play," I told him.

Lucas and Naomi wondered if she ever cooked real bacon any more.

Chapter 8

As I drove to work, my mind wandered back to yesterday. Had Jack shared the same dream in which my parents were with us or had he picked up the dream from me? Sometimes things like this drove me nuts! I would think about them far too much and would try to fit them into a framework that could be explained. I was learning that some things cannot be explained. They just *are*.

For years Lyndee, Stephanie, and I had heard stories about Ms. Abby. She had been good friends with my grandmother and had taught both my mother and Aunt Sara how to walk the Native path without compromise in the rapid pace of modern society. She was greatly loved and respected by everyone in our family, and I had heard her words quoted often in our household.

Though I had never met her, I felt her presence in the car with me. "You know that you can't put these things into a rational framework in this world. In the world of truth there is no time, space constraints, seasons, or Earthly limits. The only reason that humans box in life is that they want to control it. They fear the unknown and unseen so much that they block out everything except the here and now. When we live in the moment, free from the need to control, we see that there are many more views from so many different angles. Accepting the reality of many dimensions of existence brings with it a much richer life. That understanding makes transcending dimensions much less frightening, be it through death or dreams."

I suddenly realized that I had driven several miles out of the way and had to find a place to turn around.

"Your mind and Spirit have the capacity to be - and do - so much more than most people ever realize! Your body uses stored genetic memory to take care of many physical actions on Earth. This enables both Spirit and mind to travel to other places while your body goes about its work wherever it is. It is a fearful concept to many who would presume that we are always in control. Limited sight is an affliction that goes beyond the physical.

The places where others exist do not keep those occupants solidly in those worlds any more than we are kept here. That is why we sense them with us or smell their perfume at times.

Humans have spent countless hours trying to learn how to travel between dimensions. While that can be done, it is much easier to just let it happen naturally by accepting that our Spirits are not contained in one frail human body. Once that is understood there are no limits to this "Astral Travel," as it is sometimes called. It can, however, be a very dangerous thing. There are so many people forcing the travel that they are creating frustration, urgency, and fear in that realm. A simpler way is just to be still, be open to yourself, and always have positive thoughts. Hatred, anger, or other negative thoughts will limit the understandings of goodness and limitless existence."

Astral Travel was not a new concept for me. I had heard Aunt Sara talk about it, and at the moment it seemed simpler than the expressway I was traveling! I looked at the drivers of the vehicles flying past me and realized that very few of them were paying attention to where they were going. Most were talking on cell phones. The scene reminded me of the time I had taken Dad to the races in

Atlanta. He loved auto races and watched them on Sunday afternoons whenever he could. My sisters and I gave him tickets for Father's Day one year. Mom did not want to go and no one wanted Dad to drive, so it ended up being a road trip for just the two of us. It was a wonderful trip. Dad was out of his element, but he was so thrilled.

We were on a busy expressway then, too, with people whizzing by in a frenzy to get to wherever it was that they were going. He said they were trying to get there before it vanished. I detected a hint of sadness in his voice and glanced over to see a tear in the corner of his eye. Alarmed, I asked what was wrong. It took a few moments for him to compose himself, but when he did I was amazed at his vision.

"These people are not here," he said sadly. "They are like robots as they drive their cars. They look out into the air without expression. They do not see you as they pass or cut in front of you as they change lanes. They do not feel any other living thing as they travel. They have blank stares and empty hearts."

I looked around and for the first time realized that what he said was true. The drivers of most of the cars stared ahead with the blank stares of the dead. Now that I thought about it, these things were even more evident now than they were years ago when Dad and I made the trip to Atlanta. Everywhere I went, it seemed, there were people walking around in bodies that were merely empty shells. Their spirits just didn't seem to be there anymore. They did not see, much less feel, anyone else. Much of the time they were texting or talking on cell phones, paying no attention to their surroundings.

Ms. Abby had taught my family that the time was coming when it would be easy to identify those who could and could not hear. It seemed to me that this time had come. I had thought about it the last time I was at the mall. The aware people were moving about with ease and grace. They saw others, made eye contact easily, and smiled. They were present.

The others – those who were unaware – were rushing around, irritated at anything or anybody who was getting in their way. They grunted and huffed at the slightest need to deviate from their course.

I felt my father's presence so strongly that I found myself looking over to the other seat. "One group actually benefits from the single mindedness present in the majority. It is the subculture that exists to prey on those who do not pay attention. Crime is soaring with home invasions and robberies. Those crimes are made easy by the willing victims who refuse to be present. Having shut the door to awareness they have effectively closed off the inner voice of intuition. Some do it by taking on a false sense of self. They foolishly think they are the only ones in the world. They spend their time seeking something to make them feel whole but are looking in the wrong places. They vainly try to fill the emptiness with material things and the need to control others.

There are those who shut out the closeness of others, creating an empty place of isolation through Fear. They walk around sullenly and project an air of hardness to protect themselves from hurt."

As I pulled into my parking space at the clinic, I consciously turned my thoughts to the reality shift that I could sense was eminent. I knew that the things Mom and Dad told me were on the horizon. I could feel them. Other people could feel them, too, for they were seeking out people like Aunt Sara who heard the unseen. There was a turning of the wheel of selfishness, and I planned to do my part by pushing it forward with a unified awareness full of light and love.

I took a deep breath to center myself. Today I was working with a group of very aware physical therapists. It was so uplifting to work with them because each one was a true healer. They had taught me a great deal, and I never left feeling drained. They were masters at moving energy through themselves, only taking what they needed to transform it into something stronger before passing it on. The whole Medicine Wheel of people was represented in this one little office in our rural community. I wondered how many other little pockets of balanced healers there were in other places.

I looked forward to sharing with them my experiences of yesterday afternoon. Coming from different backgrounds, the office was a microcosm of what the world would someday be, if not in my lifetime then certainly in Jack's.

Who would have thought that I would be living and witnessing this wondrous change? Mom and Aunt Sara told me it was coming, but I never dreamed I would be around to see it! Those empty-eyed people running others down on the highways will soon be replaced by brightness and love. The power of goodness is unstoppable. All those who came and suffered but remained in the light will have their honor.

The sacrifices of the last centuries will all have been worth what we are going to see. Hope is a powerful thing. Goodness is love.

I felt energized and hopeful as I entered the building, saying my daily prayer as taught to me by Aunt Sara: "Creator, let me heal another today and transmute their pain to wholeness. Let me clearly see outside myself and be present today."

Chapter 9

I am so excited! Today we are moving into our new house! We have been working toward this day for months. What started out as really bad news has turned into such a blessing!!

I thought back to the day when the city manager knocked on our door. Brad answered the door, and I was annoyed when he invited a group of strangers into our home. I tried to ignore them and continued cooking supper while helping Jack with his homework at the table. Brad came in and whispered, "Honey, you need to come and hear what they have to say." Sensing my aggravation, Jack reached over and placed his hand on my arm. "It's okay, Mommy. They are going to make things easier." Jack interacted with at least two worlds all the time. I still saw him as a little boy even though he was about to turn ten. I turned off the stove, dried my hands, and went into the living room with a scowl and a bad attitude.

Everyone in the group stood up in mock respect and extended their hands. I not so graciously shook hands and sat down in the only vacant chair. Brad walked over and stood behind me, placing his hand on my shoulder. In our little town, everybody knew that you didn't go into somebody's house and take seats that were the obvious favorites of the home owners. Yet there sat the city manager in Brad's recliner. A stout looking woman had moved my crocheting and was sitting in my place. It was obvious from her demeanor that she was a lawyer.

"What do you want?" I asked bluntly, smiling inside in spite of myself that I sounded so much like Lyndee. The pressure increased just a little on my shoulder as Brad cringed at my abruptness. The city manager began nervously, "Mrs. Greeleaf, I have wonderful news for you and your family. The city has decided to build a new sewer processing facility that will be state of the art and have minimal impact on the environment. It will provide unfailing service for decades to come." I raised an eyebrow wondering if this man knew how silly "state of the art" and "sewer processing" sounded in the same sentence. He continued, "We are here to offer you top dollar for your home and property. Most of your neighbors have already taken our offer to purchase their property and are happily searching for their new homes."

I haven't heard a word about this from my neighbors. How did I go from homework and supper a few moments ago to losing my home to a sewer plant?

I looked at Ms. Legal in my seat, and she began to pull out a bunch of paperwork. I glanced back at the manager to see that he still wore an insincere smile. He began to speak again in syrupy sweet tones, "I know that you want what is best for our community, and for that we are willing to offer top dollar to you today for your property." The lump was growing in my throat.

These people want to build the sewer plant here where my home is! This is where we came home with Jack and where his growth marks are on the wall. This is where we have had our first holidays and birthdays. This is my sanctuary.

The room had grown silent. I did not trust myself to speak and slowly stood up. "You can all show yourself out now," I said. My voice sounded tight and strained, and I went back into the kitchen. I could hear them continue to talk to Brad in low voices as they gathered themselves to leave. I heard them say that they were leaving the paperwork with us and that they hoped we would get back to them as soon as possible. I strained to hear what they were saying. The last thing that I heard was the manager saying that the offer would only be good for 24 hours.

In a daze, I finished cooking supper and helped Jack finish his homework. We ate in silence, and when Jack asked to be excused, he came over to me. Looking me squarely in the face, he said, "Mommy, it will be better. I want to play in the barn with Russ."

Usually I found Jack's comments made sense when they were analyzed, but I was so overwhelmed with strong emotion that I barely heard him. "Not now, Jack," I said absently, still in shock and disbelief that we were about to be forced from our home.

Jack skipped off to play, and Brad started helping with the dishes. "We have to consider this, you know," he said as he hung up the dish towel.

I muttered, "I know. Let me get Jack in bed first." I went through the motions of what was usually a special time for us, resenting the committee for robbing me of those moments, too. I went downstairs to the sound of his talking to his imaginary friends.

Brad and I sat on the sofa together to read the paperwork. The bold lettering on the first page did not help my mood: Eminent Domain. I snatched the document out of Brad's hands and threw it on the floor. Brad stared at me as I jumped up and ranted about how government was not for the people anymore, that it was to oppress the people. Brad let me finish, and when I ended with a tearful, "This is our home!" he held me as I cried. Too exhausted to read or understand anything by then, he suggested that we go to bed and talk about it in the morning.

I was barely in bed before I was asleep. It was a rough night. I kept dreaming that I could hear Jack calling but that I could not find him. Brad was at work in the dream, and our house was disappearing one room at a time. Jack's voice was fading with each disappearance. I was crying in my sleep when I felt the bed give just a little next to me. I found myself somewhere between asleep and awake when I felt a gentle hand stroking my hair. I felt myself starting to settle down.

This has been your home for many years, and you have been happy here, insulated from all that was happening around you. But now your island is sinking, just like the town has been sinking for some time, in a pool of impurity. The city has grown too much too fast, and it is unsafe for you to stay here much longer.

You need to go where the air is pure and the water is clean. You need a place where Jack can grow into his full awareness – a place that is not contaminated with bad thoughts, pollution, and crime. Leave this city to its own destruction. Take the opportunity offered here and be happy.

I awoke oddly refreshed, though I found that my eyes were swollen when I looked in the mirror. I smelled coffee and wondered if Brad had been able to get any sleep. He met me on the stairs with a steaming cup and a smile. He gently put his arm around me and led me to sofa.

When I looked at him over my cup, I saw in his eyes what I already knew. He whispered, "We really have no choice if we want to retain any negotiating power." I just nodded.

Jack awoke and came running downstairs talking to someone. My cautions about running down the stairs went unheard of course.

Brad took the contracts with him and said that I should rest. "Really? You expect me to rest after all this?" He just smiled and kissed me as he went out the door. I did not watch him leave. We were taught by Mom never to watch a loved one leave. It would send the message that you might not see them come back. I don't know if that was based on a true spiritual message or if it was an old wives' tale, but I did not want to chance it. I briefly thought that maybe I should have watched the manager and his group leave the night before. Maybe I would have never seen them again.

It was my day to recharge and take care of myself. I had taken Wednesdays off ever since I started back to work. It gave me time to re-balance and get my home back in order. Today would be different with thoughts of what to do next. After getting Jack on the bus I settled down with another cup of coffee. My one cup limit did not apply after a night like the last one. I was understandably sleepy and decided to lie down for a bit.

The dream started out as all dreams do. I was just in another place. The place seemed familiar, and I was going about my daily life as though I lived there. The era was unclear as I walked from the house to the barn. I could hear a woman singing but could not understand the words. As I went toward the sound I saw an old lady shelling peas from dried hulls. She turned as I approached and smiled. This was my great grandmother! I recognized her from an old photograph in the little frame my mother kept on her dresser. She began talking to me in a language that I seemed to understand. I was comfortable pulling up a lopsided wooden stool to help her. I joined in the song and rhythm easily. We turned toward the house and saw Jack coming out with Mom and Dad. In the dream state I felt oddly normal but part of me knew that this was not right. It was as though different lifetimes were existing in the same space.

    I continued to look at the house, taking in all the details from the wooden gutters to the crooked porch. All at once I was in the kitchen of the farm house washing dishes in an old stained and pitted white sink. It was an odd piece with a corrugated drain board built into one side. I turned and began putting dishes in the dishwasher on the other side alternating between the two. Still it seemed perfectly normal.

    I did not remember the dream until a few days later when we drove into the country to look at an old farm house that was advertised as a "good investment property" and a "great fixer-upper." We drove through the weeds growing in the long driveway, and Brad laughed, saying he was afraid we had come all this way for nothing. Then we saw it. It was the farmhouse that I had seen in my dream!

    Jack cried out excitedly as he unbuckled his seat belt, "Russ!"

    Brad was saying, "Wait a minute, buddy!" but Jack was already out of the back seat and was running toward the barn. An old reddish dog with every bone showing came out of the barn to greet him. His ears perked up in spite of his condition, and it was clear that he had been expecting us. There was no containing Jack now. He rushed over to the dog, threw his arms around him, and cried,

"Russ! I told you I was coming! It will be okay now." Brad and I just looked at each other through tears. We had a lot of work to do.

So here we are, finally moving into our beautifully remodeled old farm house – with a fat, lazy, red hound dog on the porch!

Chapter 10

As I unpacked the dishes in the kitchen, I found myself lost in thought, gazing out the window and watching Jack play with Russ. His young voice drifted on the breeze through the window as he laughed and played. I briefly wondered how old the dog was. I hoped he would be here a long time.

I had been afraid that leaving the neighborhood children would leave an emptiness in Jack. I never imagined that he would be so much happier and more carefree out in the country away from his friends. Russ was his constant companion. The dog would lie on the porch snoozing all day until he heard the bus in the afternoon. He would stretch and slowly stand up, and when the bus came in sight, he would wag his tail and bark excitedly. Jack would bound off the bus and run to meet him. Every day Jack would burst through the door with Russ edging in beside him. I would point to the door and the dog would drop his head and go back to the porch where he would watch for the door to open again to signal it was once more time to play.

I was suspicious that Aunt Sara let him come inside when she was there. I was only working two days a week, but on those days, Aunt Sara was there when Jack got home. The downside was that she had to have Alex's twins ride the bus over on those days, too. It seemed a small price to pay to have Aunt Sara's help. Honestly the boys had gotten a little better with age. They were more sullen so they were not as loud. One or both were always in trouble at school. If a week passed without an incident, we were pleasantly surprised. Neither of them had any interest in anything Jack was doing and avoided him, which was all right by me. I understood why Aunt Sara had given in and gotten them both the most popular handheld video games available. When they were there, they went straight to the back room where they immediately became completely absorbed in the games.

It was spring, and I loved the way the curtains billowed over the kitchen sink as the wind passed by. The former tenants had planted old fashioned flowers around the property. Through the years they had multiplied. Now there were spots of yellow, purple, pink, and white where daffodils, hyacinths, iris, and narcissus burst joyously from their winter sleep. Patches of bright red and pink were starting to show in tulip patches here and there. The old farm was well loved, and each day brought another surprise welcoming the return of spring.

I really needed an herb garden, I thought as I continued unpacking. Ms. Abby had taught my mother and Aunt Sara all about medicinal herbs and how to grow them. I thought there might already be some growing in the yard, and I was afraid to cut down anything for fear that I would destroy a patch of something useful. We found ourselves watching each step we took outside, careful not to step on any new plant. Mom always cautioned us to take care where we tread on Mother Earth. If ever there was a mashed plant in the yard, she would care for it as though it were an injured child. "They are part of Creation, too, you know," she would tell us.

I heard a car coming up the driveway and wondered who it could be. Stepping out on the porch, I saw that it was my friends from the clinic. "We thought we would surprise you with a house warming gift," they said as I greeted them warmly. I was happy to see them but was a little confused when they brought out shovels and gloves. "We are going to plant an herb garden for you! We have brought plants from our native countries so that they can become a part of your Medicine Wheel here."

Wow! They really were listening when I spoke about our view of the universe and the Medicine Wheel!

There was no need to worry about disturbing anything that might not be showing yet. Hanako (Hana for short) fell to her knees in what looked like empty ground, exclaiming over the tiny plants that were beginning to emerge. Adrian, the Romanian physical therapist, laughed at the look on my face and explained that Hana was a highly skilled herbalist. Her name even meant "flower" in her native Japanese tongue. I was thrilled and relieved. I went over to Hana and told her that I had just been thinking about an herb garden. She smiled and touched my arm. "Your Ancestors know my Ancestors. They talk," she said simply. I was once again awestruck by the power of synchronicity and the communication of the unseen.

My friends shooed me away saying that it would not be a surprise until it was finished. I went back into the house to continue my task but could not resist peering out the window occasionally to check on their progress.

We had chosen to keep the original cabinetry in the big old kitchen. We had new doors made to replace the ones that were beyond repair. The wood was wormy chestnut and walnut, and a neighbor told us that all the wood in the house was harvested right on the property. The first owners had a small saw mill down by the creek and had milled the beautiful wood the old fashioned way. With each cabinet door I opened, I stood in the presence of all who had stood there before. It was an odd feeling. I did not care for old things and had sold most of the antiques my family did not want. It all smelled funny to me then and could not be cleaned to suit me. I regretted my decision as I stood in front of the past and felt the memory of all that was.

I heard men talking but no one was there – no one I knew or could see, anyway, but they were very present. One was saying, "They are coming. They will take everything that we do not willingly sell or give to them. I have already heard that over in Tadeaga, people had to leave with only the clothes on their backs. They left the fields ready to harvest and the fattened animals in their yards. Women were attacked and some of the young men were killed. You have to get ready, Tom. Your standing and holdings will not spare your family."

Another voice that I thought must belong to Tom said, "They will do the right thing here. We get along fine with our neighbors and our light skinned brothers. They will not harm us."

I wondered what it was all about as I closed the cabinet door. I didn't even know anyone named Tom. I opened the cabinet door again but there was nothing. Only silence.

I moved to the chair and sat for a moment looking at the cabinet. Was the house haunted? Was I hearing the breeze whispering through the old house?

I smelled the old herbs and felt a presence sit across from me. "Places hold memories, too, Marissa. Much history has passed through this house. There is no such thing as a place being haunted. That is a term thought up to bring Fear into the present about unseen events. Using Fear to move people away from a merging of worlds keeps them from knowing too much.

Here in this place you will find that there is a lot of merging. In this uncontaminated environment you will hear and see the past as it visits the here and now. Much of your new surroundings are the same as they were hundreds of years ago. The wood continues the life it began here in this place. Being a part of the living universe enables wood to carry the memories from one lifetime to the next. You will also find that each of the foundation stones has a story. Your son hears them all the time. Listen carefully to the things that you hear in this place. It is time for them to be visited in truth. It is time for the real story to be known, not the tale told by a victorious and spiteful people.

There was love, light, and happiness in this place. The imprint of those things is what brought you here. The past lives that were and are present want you to be the keeper of their truth.

Just remember that the events from the past cannot be changed. Only you can make sure that the bad things that happened do not have a place in the future. Pay attention to the mistakes that were made and use your present world to balance and correct them with goodness. Do not let the history of others decide how you view your future. Bring the wheel on around, Marissa."

I glanced around to see if anyone else had heard or seen what had just happened. The sound of laughter from the new herb garden filtered into my mind, and I heard Jack squeal in delight as Adrian sprayed him with the hose. I decided it was time to join in the fun.

When I walked outside I could not believe this was the same bare patch of Earth I had walked past just a little while ago. Hana had outlined all the plants that were poking their tiny leaves above the ground and labeled them with colorful ribbon fastened to sticks. She excitedly told me what each one was and how lucky I was to have this or that old medicine plant. She tiptoed to another section and began telling me how to use the culinary herbs. She skipped to the new section and showed me the large circle of herbs that each of them had brought from their native countries. Each one had their names and a traditional blessing from their heritage.

    I looked at this magnificent group of healers in their muddy clothes and thought that they were the most beautiful human beings I had ever seen. The glow around them was otherworldly. Because of them, my little garden of unity and hope would nourish and heal all who came near, all who tasted or smelled the herbs. This was a forever gift.

Chapter 11

In a freshly plowed field I felt the presence of my Ancestors more than anywhere else. The smell of the damp Earth, eager to support life, provoked an irresistible urge to plant, nurture, and harvest. I could hear and see Mom and Aunt Sara laughing and talking as they planted their gardens years ago.

I wanted to grow good organic food the same way that they did, and I found myself wishing I had paid more attention to what they were doing. Lyndee and I usually hurried when we were helping, and we only half listened to what they told us. Most of the time, Mom would tell us to just go on. I think secretly that was our goal – to make a big enough mess for them to send us on our way.

So here I sat with my big red dog in a small field of plowed earth, hearing the sounds of those who had cultivated here long ago. The neighbor who plowed it for me said he had plowed many a garden on this very spot. He and his dad had lived nearby all their lives. He was a good natured young man who clearly loved the earth and felt that it was a part of him.

His father stopped by to visit and see how his son was doing with their new tractor. Brad came out and joined us, looking a bit like a farmer himself. I smiled as I looked at the esteemed Dr. Greeleaf in his dirty jeans. My mother-in-law would be horrified! I turned to listen to the conversation after briefly admiring how great my husband looked in jeans.

Our neighbor was telling Brad how his family had won all the surrounding land in the land lottery of 1838. I felt the color leave my face as he said the words and felt almost as if I had been shot. His words pierced my heart like bullets. Brad realized the effect they were having on me when he saw my look of horror. I felt physically ill as father and son proudly told a tale of racism, theft, and unspeakable horror.

The two men had no idea that their words were causing me such pain. In truth, they were good souls and were very much at one with the land. Their love for the earth and its creatures was evident in the manner in which they conducted their very lives, and I knew they did not understand. I did not trust myself to speak, however, and was relieved when I heard Jack calling me.

When I reached the porch I realized that Russ had been beside me all along. He guided me now to Jack. "Thanks, Russ," Jack said quietly as he turned to me, covered in paint. "What do you think, Mom?"

Jack moved his desk chair to the center of the room and guided me to it. I realized he was talking and tried to focus. The shock was so much deeper than I realized and the effect was frightening. Jack continued to talk as though nothing had happened. I could feel that he knew what was going on and that he was intentionally trying to ground me. I was aware that Russ was now lying at my feet, but I was still unable to speak. Whenever he caught my eye he would raise his head and thump his tail on the floor.

Jack was painting his room a mushroom color. I looked at the dirty brown on his walls and wondered absently why this drab color had caught his attention. The rest of the house was painted in bright lively colors, colors that reflected the life we projected. I would not have chosen that color for him, but I knew it could have been worse. After all, I had painted my own room purple and yellow when I was thirteen.

I watch as he wiped his hands on a towel, his movements appearing in slow motion. Then he was next to me comforting me the way I had always comforted him. His words held much wisdom for a thirteen year old boy. "They are not the ones who did it, Mom. They are just people like us who love the Earth. I do not think they even know or understand what their Ancestors did, and I think they would be shocked to learn. All they know is that they were born and raised on this spot of Earth. It is as much a part of them as the hair on their heads. We are bringing the balance back by being here with them. They are willing to help out here and know that somewhere in their ancestry they must help restore balance, too. Do not hold on to the past, but let the goodness happen, Mom."

I knew Jack was right. I was just not sure how I could pretend that the past had not happened. Looking at my son, I knew that he had already let it go. He was not one to take on the hurt of others or that of the past. He understood it and moved past it leaving a smile behind. He ushered me gently past it now.

"Mushroom?" I looked at him like he was joking. He pointed to my shirt, and I saw the faint outline of his hand on my shirt. We both laughed, and I secretly vowed never to wash that shirt.

Later, after the neighbors had left, I went back out to the garden. I carried with me the ancient variety of seeds my mother had always kept in a jar. Every year she carefully harvested the best seeds from her crop. I had kept them for several years and hoped that they were still viable. As I stood looking at the freshly laid out rows, I realized that I had no idea how to plant corn or anything else for that matter. I thought about calling Aunt Sara but really wanted to do it on my own.

    As I looked around wondering where to start, I felt the smooth corn seeds in my hand. Taking a handful, I let them drop back into the jar through my fingers. It was soothing. I began to feel a surge of energy beginning in my hand and slowly moving up my arm. Then I just knew what to do. I began putting the seeds in the freshly turned ground. I vaguely wondered why I was making little mounds with three seeds in each, but it felt right. As I neared the last mound Brad appeared. "Honey, the neighbors left these seeds for you." I looked at the two little jars filled with seeds and asked if they had told him what kind they were.

    "They told me it was some kind of seed they grew every year. Their grandfather told them they were a gift from the first people who lived here."

    I felt laughter rise up from within me as I looked down at the seeds of my Ancestors, housed in those two little jars. I felt Ms. Abby near.

    "Good seeds never die. They lie dormant sometimes while they wait for a gentle hand to coax them back to life. These men unknowingly kept the good seeds from your people alive and viable. They have come back full circle. Their ancestors might have taken the land but they kept the important things alive until the time they could be returned.

    Each seed represents a life. The life of the plant it carries is unique. The genetic structure is similar but there is always a slight difference. The ancients knew this and always saved seeds from several different plants to keep the seeds healthy.

The seeds you hold in your hand are the offspring of the original plants given to your Ancestors. They have gone though many seasons. They remember the hands that helped them. They remember the harvest and the people who tended them. They weathered late freezes and summer winds that knocked them to the ground. They bravely got back up and continued their task to provide life through giving their own lives.

Each of them represents a conscious decision to save and preserve. Each one is given the honor to gift life once more."

I gently took out the precious seeds and marveled at their size. They were bigger than any at the seed store. I instinctively knew what to do with them. Brad asked if he could help, but I knew that I was the one who needed to touch each of them and give them to the fertile ground to grow and mature to nourish our family.

I moved carefully back through the mounds of corn. In each mound I added the squash and beans. About half way through the planting I was singing a song that I don't remember learning. Intent on my planting I did not realize that Stephanie had come over until I heard her voice in perfect pitch join me in song. I looked up at her and smiled. She sat down at the edge of the garden and continued to sing. The song grew, and I realized that the wind was taking the song and circling it back to us with the intensity of many voices.

As I finished planting, I heard the ending note ~ ski ~ echo through the air.

GY Brown and PH Jones

Chapter 12

Summer soon became my favorite time of year. Going outside to get supper was the most wondrous blessing. I had not really appreciated what a labor of love the food was when I was growing up. Mom and Aunt Sara worked in the garden from spring to fall. During the winter months they planned the next garden and worked on seeds. There would be little pots everywhere with tiny plants sprouting. Every day I heard them exclaiming over the newest sprouts. To us girls it was just pots of dirt everywhere. Now I understood.

Giving life to the tiny seeds was akin to giving birth. As I took the tiny seeds in my own fingers, I too felt the wonder that made my mom smile. I felt the peacefulness of being a part of something much bigger than myself. I was one with all my Ancestors who had held a tiny seed and had envisioned the fruit of that seed on the table nourishing a family.

This was a tradition as old as time. It transcended all racial, religious and geographic lines. Seeds were the birth of hope. They had been used in many different ways throughout history. Some of the ways were not so honorable. Wars waged against people who depended on their harvest were timed to destroy the harvest. The attackers knew that destroying all hope of winter food could very well vanquish the enemy. What they did not count on was that the survival mechanism of the seed was as strong as it was in humans. Often the seeds would flourish in the ashes becoming stronger and rising like a Phoenix.

I drifted back to when Mom would tell us about the first seed. This first seed did rise out of ashes. The original tobacco of the Native people was a hardy plant. It had to be nourished by females and gifted to males. This first herb was considered Sacred to my people and had to be given life properly.

I smiled as a soft breeze brushed my face. My Ancestors were gently reminding me of their presence. I could hear the story of healing herbs begin, only this time it was a different voice. Mom would say, "This is how Ms Abby told me medicine herbs came to be."

"There was a time when all of Creation worked together for the greater good. The humans and the animals counted on each other for wit and strength and each did what they did best. No one was strained or tired. The strong Bears did the hard labor, the Humans figured out the best way to do things and planned for the community. The women took what the other animals gathered and made use of it all. Everyone was happy.

One winter the human men grew lazy. They did not want to go out into the cold to carry out their tasks. They got together and used their wit to find a way to make the much stronger Bears do their work. They thought that they were smarter than the Bears. After a little while the Bears grew tired of being the ones to carry more than their share of the physical burden of the community. They got together and decided that they would leave the humans and organize their own community. They knew they had to do this because they were becoming angry and could hurt or kill the humans if pushed too far.

The human men were angry over this decision. They had grown even lazier with the Bears doing their share of the work. The men began to use force to make the weaker women do the hard work. The women were becoming broken and were in pain much of the time. Their children suffered because they were not able to nurture them properly. One day the women stopped to rest as they were dragging meat home. They heard the plants speak. The Plant People had been watching the way the women were treated and decided to help them.

First the Willow spoke, "Take my bark and chew a piece of it to ease your pain." The women were startled and looked at each other in fear. As they huddled closer, other plants began to talk in a way they could understand. Each one told the women how to use it to heal and comfort. The plants told the women that they would always be within reach when they needed them. They also told them how the plants should be gathered.

When the plants finished sharing their knowledge, the women asked what they could do for the plants in return for this Sacred knowledge. The plants instructed the women not to share this knowledge with the men. To do so would mean that they would abuse the plants and create harm from them. They told the women to always offer something in return as a thank you to the plant. Also they were never to take more than they needed at that moment. Each offering of thanks would show the plants that the women remembered.

To ensure that the plants would be used in a good way, they agreed on a method of telling the plant how it was going to be used and for whom. This would be a secret pact between the plant and the women. Should the men see or hear what plant the women were using and abuse it, the plant would not heal. The sacred words were the way to open the healing power.

The women were relieved to have Medicine. Their pain was eased as they chewed the tangy bark from the Willow. They used its leaves to wrap their broken and strained bodies. Soon they were laughing and dancing. Moving without pain was a great blessing.

The women realized that they had been gone a very long time, and they were worried that they might be beaten for taking so long. A plant which aided sleep spoke up, "Take my roots and make a tea for the men tonight. They will sleep for a while and give you time to grow stronger."

The women returned to the village to the sound of angry voices. They told the men to drink the tea while the meat cooked. Soon the men were sound asleep. The women and children ate all they wanted. They had been hungry for a long time. There was laughter once more in the village.

The men woke to a balanced existence. They did not understand how things had changed, but they knew things were different. They did not beat the women or starve their children any longer. They honored the women as healers and life givers. Their hearts were open once more to the balance."

I smiled as I thought about Lyndee's comment after first hearing this story. "I bet they were scared to abuse anybody after that - they knew they could just as easily make that sleep permanent!" Mom reminded Lyndee that we were healers and life givers, not life takers. Stephanie and I stifled giggles at the face Lyndee made in response.

I felt true peace and a sacred connection to those women long ago as I looked out at my herb garden. I knew what each plant was and how to use it for good. My gaze wandered to the field and woods. Aunt Sara had come over weekly to walk with me and help me identify the plants that grew here. She was excited to find so many of the old plants growing nearby.

I noticed that Aunt Sara was getting a little slower during our walks. I needed to give more thought to making a place for her to be near us as she got older. She needed to be near her family, and she needed to be in a place where she would be able to feel the Earth.

As I was wondering what would be the best thing to do, I glanced across our little pond. I had not been down there much because we had not had time to work in that area. I blinked several times as an old cabin seemed to become superimposed over the weeds. My curiosity aroused, I moved to get a better look. As I drew near, I could hear girls laughing and women talking. What was this place? I had accepted that the other dimensions and planes of existence merged often here. There was nothing frightening about that anymore. I actually found it comforting to know that those who had left the Earth walk still visited and guided me here.

I could see the cabin more clearly as I was guided toward it by forces I could not see. It had a large porch with women sitting in rockers doing handwork. I walked up on the porch amidst greetings and smiles. They knew me! The door was open and I just walked in. There sat my great-grandmother, sewing a quilt with the other women. The quilt was on a big wooden frame hanging from the ceiling by ropes. She motioned for me to join them.

This is extraordinary! It is good to be here in this woman's place.

I looked at the herbs drying in ribbon tied bunches along the wall. I recognized the quilt she was working on as the same now- raggedy quilt that was in my cedar chest.

I was brought back to the present by Russ who was licking my face as I sat on the ground in the weeds. I batted my eyes and adjusted to the current dimension. What a blessing to be able to feel the imprint of the good things that were here in this place. I glanced around and saw several stacks of stones spaced at intervals of approximately five feet. This was where a house had been!

Now I know what this is! This is the place where the neighborhood women came once a month to be away from the daily labor of farm life! I always heard that we separated ourselves during our moon time. Now I know that it was so that we could rest and do things we liked to do with other women. This is a place of camaraderie and laughter!

Russ's insistence that I return to the house made me aware that it was almost time for Jack to be home. As I returned I was already planning the little cabin that we would soon build for Aunt Sara.

Chapter 13

I was more than a little perplexed by Aunt Sara's call. All these years I had been learning the old way and hearing our Ancestors. I thought that I was already doing what the women from our heritage were supposed to do. So Sara's tone and words seemed out of the ordinary when she said, "You are going to have to step up and lead not only the family but the rest of creation. It is time for me to pass on the things I know to you." Had she heard something about her health that she had not shared with us?

I started some water for tea and thought of all the herbal and healing knowledge I had gained in my lifetime. I had learned from many people, not just Aunt Sara. Hana had taught me about Asian herbs, and Adrian had taught me the herbs and remedies his grandmother in Romania had used when he was a young boy. Cecily completed the Medicine Wheel by teaching me about the bush remedies in her native Africa. I thought it was interesting and wonderful that the four of us had been brought together. We all used the body's energy to heal. Whether it was called Life Force, Heat, Aura, Chi, or Prana, it was the same thing. Our sameness drew us together for the greater good, the healing and giving of life.

I thought about our beginnings as a people and our original instructions. We began as one people. The universe wanted us to know more about the important things of which we were a part so we were divided into four groups. Each group was given an element to study and protect. Our instructions were to learn everything we could about our element and how it could be used for the good of all. We were given the things we needed to be comfortable while we were learning.

At the end of our learning time, we were charged to come together as one people and share our knowledge with one another. The Medicine Wheel would be our reminder of our Sacred mission. It was divided into colors and quadrants. Each quadrant held a people who would have smaller Medicine Wheels to guide them and remind them of the whole. My People were given Earth to keep and care for. We were to learn all that we could about the Earth and the medicines she grew. Cecily's People were given Water to learn and understand. Hana's ancestors were given Air. They learned about the medicine from air and how to use it to heal. Adrian's people were given Fire. After we mastered these lessons we would come together and learn from each other. I was blessed to have the completion of this sacred order in front of me so clearly.

The sound of Aunt Sara's car brought me back to the present. I went to the door and saw that she was gathering things from her car. As I went out to help her, I wondered why she had her ceremonial items with her. I stepped back while she gathered them. No one touched the Sacred or Ceremonial items of a medicine person unless handed them by the person. Needless to say I was a bit shocked when she thrust her basket towards me. I looked at her before taking the basket, and what I saw was a look I had never seen before. It was a far away kind of look, but not a view of a past memory. It was something else – something I didn't quite understand.

I expected the basket to give some kind of surge or something, considering what was in it. It was no different than carrying a sack of groceries, and that surprised me.

Aunt Sara called out from the back of the car, "The power is not in the basket, child. It is in knowing what the basket holds."

    I always wondered how she did that. It was a common thing that both she and my mother did - answering an unasked question. Sometimes they answered the question before it had fully formed in my mind. That made growing up around these extremely gifted women something of a challenge. Getting away with anything was a joke! We soon learned that when we thought we were getting away with something, it was just because they felt sorry for us and pretended not to see or know. When we figured it out, that took some of the fun out of it for us. I personally thought, however, that Lyndee surprised them a couple of times with things that they did not see coming.

    A stout "hea-na" drew me back to the task at hand. "Hea-na or "hea-ah" were universal commands that even the animals knew. It meant here-now - and I mean now!

    We took everything into the house and sat down for a cup of tea. I noticed that Aunt Sara's hands were trembling slightly, and I asked if she was all right. After a few moments she said, "Yes, I am okay. It is just hard to know where to start. Even though I know this is the right thing to do, I am prayerfully asking that the right words be given to me."

This is scary! I've never heard Aunt Sara talk this way. She is never nervous and is the one who is always in control. What is this thing she is about to do?

    Aunt Sara resolutely set down her cup and began. "When Ms. Abby taught your mother and me the things we needed to know to carry on the traditions, she gave each of us specific duties or ceremonies. Your mom had to give me hers to keep until I found the right person to pass them to. She had begun teaching them to your cousin Mandy and was hopeful that she could turn them over to her. That was not to be, however, because Mandy became heavily involved in drugs. Naomi was sad about that the rest of her days. She always worried that she had chosen the wrong person and that the weight of responsibility might have been what drove Mandy to drug use.

There was no doubt that Mandy had the gifts and could carry out the ceremony, but maybe her mind was not strong enough. Naomi grieved Mandy's crossing long before she physically crossed over, and she grew fearful to pass the gifts and responsibilities to another young woman since she faulted herself for choosing Mandy and blamed herself for what happened. There was nothing I could say to ease Naomi's heartache from that even though she fully understood that Mandy's life agreement was written by her and that there was likely nothing we could have done to change the events that happened.

I always thought that Mandy played Naomi like a drum, tricking her into thinking that she was the one who could carry on the traditions. I saw that Mandy could be selfish and manipulative and was doubtful that she would embrace any sacred responsibility. There could be no hint of selfishness in any Tradition Keeper, and I saw what your mother did not see – self-indulgence and greed."

This must be why Aunt Sara is trembling so much. She must be struggling with a choice much like the one Mom had to make. She must be here to ask my opinion about who could best carry on her work.

Sara continued. "Our Traditions are not lost as long as one person remembers. Our Medicine ways and Ceremonies have been passed down quietly throughout time. They have never been written down since it is forbidden to write the Sacred. The only way these things stay true to Tradition is that each person giving them only give them as they were received without altering them. The receiver must never add to them or leave anything out." After a pause she continued. "Keepers of Tradition seek the right individuals to give them to from the time we accept the responsibility. We know that these things are never truly ours until we give them away. We watch a person from childhood to determine who is best suited for the task. We observe how they develop and how they respond to events in their lives. I cannot pass your mother's responsibilities to you because it is forbidden to pass these things directly through our own children."

My mother had told me that she would not be able to pass all of her knowledge on to me because of a piece of history told to her by Ms. Abby. All she would tell me was that teachings kept in one family had created problems in the past and that she would have to pass the Traditions to someone other than me or Stephanie.

Remembering this story enabled me to understand Aunt Sara's apprehension. The weight of responsibility rested on her not only to pass on her traditions but also to pass on those of my mother.

This also explained why Sara was so easily frustrated with Lyndee. It was clear to me now that she had hoped to give Mom's responsibilities to her. The fact that Lyndee had never settled down to become a Life Giver had been a true source of pain for Sara. Being the loose cannon that Lyndee was, it would just be too risky to pass along such responsibility to her.

Lyndee had developed her own gifts, however, apart from the traditions. And though they were completely different, they were by no means less valued. Lyndee had taken on a warrior Spirit with beauty. She was a healer in her own right. If there was anyone who could be trusted to protect and fight for those who were chosen to keep the Traditions – it was Lyndee!

Aunt Sara began to talk as she slowly and with reverence took her basket and began taking the items out.

"This Basket belonged to Ms Abby, Marissa. It was given to her by her teacher who was a very knowledgeable Medicine Woman. The basket is made from the same river cane that was given to the people to make tools and weapons. It is made twice and woven together as one which symbolizes the unity of humans with the rest of Creation. The colors in the basket are made from out traditional herbal dyes. Each color represents a sacred plant that gave its life for this cause. Each one was chosen for the medicine it gives to the circle of life. Like the Wampum Belts of our brothers the Haudenosaunee, the woven pattern in the basket tells a story. This design tells the story of the first Medicine Lodge."

Aunt Sara continued taking out her Sacred items, explaining each of them in detail. She told me that each piece held the memory of all the experiences it had been a part of as well as the life that it had before it became what it is now. I found myself looking at them through tears many times during her discourse. My understanding deepened as did my appreciation of all the parts of Creation that came together permitting us to have access to the Sacred.

Each element, each color, each direction and season were all represented. Each life form in the universe was here in this basket. I felt the energy from it warming the table. I saw Aunt Sara's face relax into a smile as she saw that the understanding was coming to me.

"It is not that a basket has any power. A basket made from living things, however, is given life through honoring Sacred life, and that makes the basket powerful. Earlier you picked up a basket that was mine. You did not know its story. Now you know the story and the life that is in this basket. You will never look at a basket the same way." I knew she was right. The life emanating from the basket was a powerful force that I had not felt earlier.

"It is time, Marrisa, for you to begin to do what you were chosen to do. Your child is nearly grown and does not need your full attention. Your home is settled and does not require your constant supervision. It is time for you to give back energy to the universe so that the blessings can continue. You must now expand your healing to beings and places you may never know. It is time for you to give yourself to a higher purpose.

You will take on the suffering of the innocent and transform it into a moment's peace. You will make whole the shattered children and trapped Elders from a distance. You will vision for those who can't see. You will hear for those who can't understand. Your life is now part of a greater destiny. These are the things for which you have been prepared. This is where everything you have felt, done, seen, heard, known and experienced come together. You will be the one who remembers and holds these teachings until you can give them away. When you have reached the point of giving them away, they will become truly yours, and the great peace that comes with that will reside forever in your Spirit."

PART III

Jack

GY Brown and PH Jones

Chapter 1

The journey started out like all other lives do:

- ✓ Hear that it is time to be formative.
- ✓ Realize what I need to learn by conferring with Spirit.
- ✓ Absorb the Knowing as I am given the lessons I have yet to learn.
- ✓ Gather the things I need for this journey.
- ✓ Prepare my Spirit for entry.

Wait. Something is different. You want me to use this among the humans? Are you sure they are ready and won't try to destroy me?

This was going to be a trip to remember. I was actually going to be able to keep the Knowing with me from the beginning this time. I would have to forget some things, of course, to function as a human, but for the most part it would all stay with me this time. It was exciting!

Now I need to find a family whose members have some awareness. They will have to understand that the things I am bringing with me are for the greater good. These things are gifts for the universe, not just for the family I will choose.

My family needed to be in the middle with mixed blood lines and a wide circle of influence. They had to be aware enough to protect me from attempts to drug and change me while I was young. I needed people who were accepted easily and listened to by others. Above all else, there had to be at least one member of the family who clearly heard the Knowing already.

This one looks interesting. She is an intuitive healer. He is still learning but has a position in the medical community that affords respect. They look kind. She even turns and looks towards me as I am inquiring. She is aware! I will look around just a bit more, but these people are on the list for sure.

There was another possibility, a family with whom I initially felt I could have a nice experience. The weather was nice all the time where this other family lived, and that was important. The last one had been freezing, and if possible I didn't want to be cold all the time. I discounted them, however, as soon as I saw my prospective father slap my prospective mother. That would never do as it takes everything out of a Spirit. My mission was too important to get tied up in that kind of battle. I would be recommending another one for them, though. I had just the right one in mind.

Geez! There are still so many unhappy people here! I would have thought that they had grown so much more in the time I have been away. I would have liked to enter a culture already living with the Knowing. Didn't I do this one already?

I decided to go with the first family I had considered. The first one was usually the right one anyway.

This is nice. I like the way she is singing to me. I feel the Knowing growing stronger in this family. The music is good for my evolution. It is nice to see that this group knows that we can hear them clearly in utero. I like the way the man puts his smiling face near me when he talks, too. "Hey, there! Do you like the sound of that?"
This mother massages me! It feels good and helps me not be so sore from all this growing. Yes, this is nice. We get to listen to that other lady sing and play, too, which is definitely something to consider.

This mother took very good care of herself. I was getting the proper nutrition as well as plenty of rest. It made my formation much easier. The last one ate way too much spicy food and was surrounded by smoke all the time. It is no wonder that my breathing apparatus never formed correctly and that it soon failed. What did they think would happen with all those bad things filtering in to me? Still I felt sad for her. She had forgotten too much and then tried to follow me. I tried to tell her to go back, but she kept on until she was forced to start over.

I wondered if they knew that this grandfather had almost finished his contract. He knew, but he still told me about the things we were going to do together. As his mind drifted closer to my recent world, I told him that I would take his love and hold onto it for the family he was so reluctant to leave. His Spirit knew things were changing. He gave me his knowing from this family. He had led a good life and had managed to change a lot of hurt into something good. My love for this Spirit was eternal. We had traveled the same path before, and though our kinship had changed through the lives, our unconditional love remained.

Oh, good grief! Settle down! Lucas is only going to rest and recuperate from his human experience for a while. I know that all of you are aware of this transition and have been prepared to help him through it. I will make my grand entrance and distract you from the momentary blindness which is afflicting you right now. Catch up with you later, Lucas!

I came to this family in a time of confusion. The confusion was not localized, either. There was confusion everywhere. There were wars for unknown causes and famine far more widespread than was commonly known. Governments all over the planet were oppressing Creation, trying to stomp down the awareness that was growing stronger and stronger. Mother Earth was changing, too. She was shifting and trying to recover from the damage and disease inflicted by the humans.

We were all coming in for one reason -The New Era. This would be the Era that would change everything. Our Spirits gave this information to those closest to the Remembering, the ones who never closed their ears and taught the truth through the generations. They had been telling the others what was coming for a while. Some had even written it down on the counting tablet. It took a very, very long time for the others to hear them. Finally they did, and now many were worried that Creation would cease to exist.

My comrades and I will lead you through these changes to a better world. You will see! Everything will be known. No one will be able to hide. Intentions will open dialogs and leave no room for selfish verbal manipulations. Truth will be seen clearly, and there will be no more "double talk"

We will show you that there is no fear. You will remember your life agreement. Those who insist on oppression will lose all power.

Your shield from harm will be universal love. We will exist in a state of peace. We will not give evil, envy, greed, or hate anything to help it grow. We will gently move aside when negativity visits, leaving it alone with itself.

Wake up! We are here and ready for the adventure!

Chapter 2

It was nice for Mom to finally be holding me in her arms, stroking my head with a soft caress. This was one of those really good things that we get to experience as humans - The Soft Touch. Dad was just watching us.

I don't think that I need the full seven days to make this decision! I am sure that this is the family with whom I want to spend this lifetime. We have interacted many times in other worlds, at different times, and on different planes. This is my family. I have carried all the things that they forgot through time immortal. They will remember this time much more than the other times.

It is funny how Mom and Dad got together this time. They were both headed in different directions for a while. Looking at them now it was hard to imagine how close they had come to missing this part of their journey here. It would have made things a lot harder if they had continued in those other directions, but it would not have changed this moment. The mishap in the journey would have been righted eventually. There would have been some negative feelings left behind when they left the wrong paths. The wrong relationships would have healed, though, and they would have gotten back on track with their life agreements.

It was good to see Gloria back here, too. She had never fully committed to a life. Maybe she would be able to do it this time, after she understood what I was here to show her. There was so much that she had pushed to the back of her memory. She kept filling her mind and spirit with empty trinkets that could not hold the Spirit. She would remember, and she would grow forward this time. I would help her get there so that there would be no need for her to go backward- again.

I wondered where her husband had wandered. He was a piece of work with so many secrets and too many alternative lives he attempted to live at once. Of course Gloria never told him that he was not Brad's biological father. I saw that she had even forgotten that herself. There was already so much distance between them that it could not be narrowed - not in this lifetime, anyway.

There he was, sticking his head in the door and saying all the right words, then adding his typical, "Gotta run! Duty calls!" I saw that Gloria had perfected her plastered smile as she turned away. She had dealt with so many things before by turning away.

She knows. I will give her the courage to be a whole person. Let him do what he does, and let her feel that she deserves it for now. That is all about to change. There will be no hiding from oneself or the world this time around.

Oh, my gosh! Do I really have to go through this infancy thing again? This is the hardest part to me - all these strangers poking and prodding. Enough already! I am ready to go home and get started on this life.

The voice of Knowing echoed throughout the universe: *"Not so fast! You know the rules. In seven human days you can make that call. Not sooner, not later."*

Okay. I'll wait. But I do already know what my decision will be.

As we prepared to leave the hospital, I realized how funny Dad was - so worried about the cars and the weather. I wanted to tell him it was going to be fine. I wondered idly where Lainy was. We had agreed to do this together but I couldn't see her. Maybe she was running late or had to take care of something before making her entrance.

I knew that I should be watching the life story I was accepting, but I felt a stronger pull to take the sorrow from Mom right now. She had forgotten that Lucas was not far. He would be the Ancestor that she will hear on the wind. I moved my thoughts to Lucas, asking him to comfort her. He instantly did, and her voice changed from broken words to whole sentences.

"Do we need to stop by the funeral home and make arrangements before we go home?" she was asking Dad. His answer was sweet and tender, "You don't need to do a thing, Honey. Steph and Lyndee are taking care of everything you discussed." Mom settled back and closed her eyes for a moment.

It's okay, Mom. He is right here with us. Look back here at me, and you will feel better.

Marissa – that's my Mom's name - glanced back to look at me just as a tear escaped down her cheek. "I don't know what I'll do with Dad gone forever," she said. "It is just like him to turn his passing into something else, like a birthday. How far in the other direction he took us this time to beat sorrow down! I am sure that I heard him in the room as Jack was being born." Dad just nodded and squeezed her hand.

When we arrived at the house called home, I noticed something was different. I didn't remember that awful buzzing sound I heard as we got out of our vehicle. It sounded dangerous to me. I looked around and saw that there were very big power lines nearby.

What could you be thinking? Those things will kill us, and we will all have to start over! Hasn't anyone figured out yet how deadly they are to all life forms? You can clearly see that the trees and grass are trying to stay away from them. No wonder Aunt Lyndee is going to get so sick that I have to take care of her. The things that people do will always be odd to me. They lose so much when they agree to forget. Not to worry, though, because we are about to change all that!

My parents placed me gently in my crib. There was much work to do in the dream world and so many things to understand.

Let's get started so that I can make an informed decision. Ok, everyone - come in and take a look at me. Then go on about your business while I go about mine.

I heard Mom talking to Dad and listened carefully. "Brad, look how he watches us. Are you sure that they cannot see well when they are this young?"

Dad looked intently for a moment. I squirmed, trying to get our communication online to tell him that I can see just fine. I was having to switch between the world I just left, the world here, and the future one, all combined in a universal view at the same time. Panoramic does not even begin to describe it! But I could see just fine.

"They can't focus at this age, but they can see black and white, shadows, and that kind of thing." I laughed out loud at that. My dad was a funny guy!

We can see so much at this point. Our vision actually fails as we forget. I will be showing you a different way to remember soon enough. For now, you may hold onto your old wives' tales.

As the room grew quiet, I began viewing my new life's story. This life was a very loving one. The family had experienced loss and heartache, but they had gotten through it together. That was good.

Mom was quite the lady, and she was very sharp. Dad was every bit a gentleman who loved us with all his being. There was a wonderful group of aunts, but I wasn't so sure about the uncles and grandfather. They seemed to have agendas hidden from even themselves. They did not appear to be too involved in my task. Sadly I saw that they were going to have to redo this one. It looked like the thing they were here to do was to get my dad here. His brothers were just very empty. I wouldn't even know them this round because they were too involved in material things to see Spirit. They would become part of the invisible mass of humanity waiting for the train to the next existence.

I saw that I was going to be the child who was picked on a bit in school. I knew that it would not be a problem because I had already been the bully in one life. That was really hard because it was against my nature. I was the observer who did nothing in another life, and I was the onlooker who came forward and changed it in yet another. This would complete that experience so I was ready for it.

I started seeing other events that were part of this life.

WOW, this looks great! I get to help others feel better. The best part is that I don't really even have to try since it is part of my nature. I get to keep the peacefulness that I came with and just let it drift around me. This is going to be a good life. I see that I get to keep the healing knowledge and that my Star Friends will always smile at me. I do not have to forget their names this time! Yay! The Rock People will keep me company all the time. I will be able to carry them in my pocket whenever I want.

Making friends with other people was going to be hard, I saw - at least until I was able to find others like me. I really wouldn't need them for a while as long as the Star and Rock People were with me. Relationships on this level were hard to maintain.

It was much easier to go with the relationships that we came with instead of having to make them as we went along. It seemed to me that there was always someone wanting to create a relationship where there should not be one. It created a lot of problems when these forced relationships ended. Someone always got hurt, and I tried to avoid that whenever I could.

I saw that my sympathies were abused a lot. I sure hoped that I could remember not to get drawn into the dramas that Unawares loved so much. There really was no need for all that. Life would be what it would be. People would no longer be able to hide behind the drama because all would be known.

I saw that many did not even try to hide. If they were not going to hide, why did they need us to be there to rip down the curtain, showing what is behind it? I wasn't sure I understood.

I saw that I was going to have to be stronger than most and be the sounding board for much older and wiser people. Many of the aware people would come to know me and continue to communicate as we do without bodies. I would have to be an example for others.

No matter what happened, I knew I must stop it when others tried to impose their life agreements onto me. This was the time when many would try and it would not be allowed. I would have the right to defend my life agreement at all cost and defend others who needed assistance to protect their awareness.

Be very aware and watchful of false teachers. Pay special attention to those that others are trying to silence or oppress. The loudest ones shout to cover the voices of truth. Be the champion for silence, stillness, softness, and kindness. When you see any of these being pushed aside, reach over and pull them back. The good things that have already happened must be kept in the light. Do not let darkness fall on the good progress.

Do not let others worry over you if you don't eat or sleep like they do. You will have a different rhythm and will not need the same kind of nourishment the ones before you needed. You will also have to be sure that you do not deny your gifts. Even when it is hard and you would rather be silent, you must not turn away or cower in your differences.

Chapter 3

As time speeds up, you will slow down. As the world spins forward, you will dance backward. When too much is being used, you will stop using. As the seasons turn contrary, you will be content. As the stars shine brighter you will remember their names.

"Hurry, Brad! I don't want him to miss the eclipse! There won't be another one for five hundred years."

I wondered why Mom was so worried about that. I knew when every eclipse was going to happen. I guess she was worried that her life agreement would not be complete unless she provided me opportunities to see everything I could. They had already positioned my bed so that I could look at all my Star friends as I fell asleep.

On this particular night, I couldn't resist teasing my parents. I slipped downstairs quietly and stood at the living room window. I could hear Dad running around upstairs, calling out to Mom that he could not find me. It was so hard to be quiet, standing there behind the curtain. I watched as Aunt Stephie and Aunt Lyndee built a fire for roasting marshmallows, and I heard the change in their voices as they began calling my name. I realized that they knew I was playing.

Suddenly Dad was there. He scooped me up, curtain and all, and made me laugh. "Come on, Sport. Your mom wants you to see something." I ran to my rocks and stuffed as many as I could into my pockets before going outside.

The first person I ran to was Aunt Lyndee. I loved the way she would toss me in the air, making my mom gasp and my dad laugh. Lyndee was the best aunt for playing. She was, in fact, one of the reasons I wanted this life. She gave so much of herself to others. She was my protector just like she had always been Mom's and Aunt Stephie's. They loved to tell me stories about her – especially the one about the time she rescued Aunt Stephie from a guy in grade school who was harassing her.

After playing with Lyndee, I ran over to Aunt Stephie who was already sitting in a lawn chair. She was such a gentle spirit and gave the best hugs of anybody. I could feel her love surround me like the purest of lights.

Mom laid quilts on the ground so we could lie on them and watch the sky. I was much more interested in the fire. Dad was telling Lyndee how to tend the fire, but of course Lyndee was doing it the way she thought it should be done, paying little attention to him. I could tell that Lyndee often wondered why she was sharing life with him. They were not from the same universe at any time. This was actually the first time they had crossed paths. She had a habit of asking him what planet he was from. He always made a weird sound when she did, and everyone else would hide their smiles.

Stephie got out the sticks and put marshmallows on them. She handed me a stick and stood by the fire, showing me how to cook them. I let her tell me all about it and giggled thinking about all the other times I had cooked food on an open fire. But to make them all feel good, I would have fun with this. It was more fun to catch them on fire and watch them turn black and melt. I liked the way they tasted when they were burned, too.

Just then I saw Myka run across the sky. I squealed excitedly and clapped my hands. He was the most fun to run with in the sky, and he always left blue streaks along his path that made people say, "Ahhhh!" and "Ohhhhh!" Mom tried to get me to lie down, but that was not going to happen. Not with Myka to play with!

Myka, where is everyone else?

No sooner had I asked than the others came. They were running across the sky, laughing and throwing colors everywhere. They were very happy to see me. Myka said they were particularly happy that I remembered their names and the good things we could do together. His mother soon moved closer and spoke to me: "We are going to be closer to you down there as time passes. We are getting ready to use the old paths we made a while ago."

My body was getting tired so I went to rest on one of the quilts for a while and watch Grandmother Moon. We always gave her the greatest respect. She took care of so much that I wondered if she were tired. She had to take care of the water as well as the Moms and her Star Children. She made sure people did not get lost and could keep track of time. I wondered if the grownups ever thought about all she did.

Why doesn't Grandmother Gloria do things for other people and help keep up with things? Isn't that what Grandmothers do - take care of things?

That question went unanswered, and I must have fallen asleep because I awoke to Mom's saying, "Look,

Baby! Grandmother Moon is almost hiding. Watch her peek out in a few minutes!" I smiled and cuddled with Mom. She was so sweet and tried to give me all kinds of different experiences. One day I would be able to show her different things, too. I began dozing in her arms and was soon chasing Myka behind other stars.

Chapter 4

Being around other children at daycare was fun. I loved the way they remembered, too. Lainy was there – a blonde this time – and I was glad to see her. I had been wondering about her. "Hey, Lainy! Glad to see you made it here. I have had a hard time finding you!"

What's this? She is looking at me the way the Unawares do- with only mild curiosity. Lainy! It's me! Oh, no. She forgot! How is that possible? I'll try sending thought-words, very slowly…….. Still nothing!

Some of the other children responded. I didn't know why Lainy had forgotten, but I was happy that I was not alone. I scanned the room and heard others like me. It was going to be just fine. There were more children who heard thought-words than who didn't so that was good. I knew I would have to get on the ball with Lainy, though. There were several things that we needed to finish together. I went over to her again, but she backed up without hearing or recognizing me.

One of the teachers could hear and was always smiling at us. Thank goodness Mom was able to find a place with at least one aware adult. That had made things much easier. The kind lady who could hear called us to snack time. She apologized in thought-words and encouraged us to play along as she put out some kind of cheese cardboard and colored sugar water. She placed less in front of those like me so that at least we didn't have to eat large quantities. When we were finished, she scooped up what we just could not eat and quickly discarded it so that the other adults didn't see that we had not consumed our portions.

I really liked this lady. She seemed right on the mark with her knowing. She heard and saw us, and that was comforting. As the day went on I watched her catch children before they fell, turn and distribute items without being asked, look at one who was looking at her from another area, and do many other little things that told me she was very much in tune. She was one of the leaders who had made this round of life possible. Without her and her kindness we would not have stood a chance. She was pretty, too, and had the same clear blue eyes that we did.

Playtime came, and I feared we were once again going to be misunderstood. Ms. Pretty Eyes sent us another silent apology along with instructions to pretend to be like the others for a while. "Pick a toy and act interested. 'Oooh' and 'Ahh' over it and bang it on the floor."

I laughed aloud this time. Seriously? Bang it on the floor? I looked around and saw that this was exactly what the other children were doing - Aware and Unaware alike! I had a hard time watching a kid trying to force a round peg into a square hole. I was going to show him how to do it and help relieve his frustration, but just as I was doing so the other lady grabbed my arm and roughly moved me to another area. I didn't understand why she seemed so upset. She was also mumbling something that I didn't understand.

I looked around for some clue that might explain what had just happened. Everyone seemed to be busy at their play, not even noticing me. Then one of children whispered, "Just play along. That adult thought you were trying to take the toys away. She didn't know you were just trying to help." That explained it. But now I didn't know what to do.

If something so minor as that can get me snatched up, maybe I should just lie down! What? That isn't permitted, either?

The other lady picked me up and returned me to the play area. This was going to be much more difficult than I had imagined. I looked toward the others and realized that they had tuned out. They appeared to be like the Unawares, talking garble and acting like robots. How did they do it? Ms. Pretty Eyes worked her way back to me. She smiled reassuringly and told me that I would grow accustomed to it.

The strangest and most cruel ritual happened at story time. I did so love to hear Ms. Pretty Eyes read stories! She read with such expression, and she used funny voices that brought the stories alive. She kept us pretty much spellbound the entire time. The problem was that we were expected – no, <u>forced</u>! - to sit cross-legged on the floor without moving the entire time.

I wanted to hear the story, and I wanted to please Ms. Pretty Eyes more than anything. It's just that I found it impossible to keep the small body to which I had been assigned perfectly still for that long. I mean, I just could not do it! The body needed to move, and I found that I had very little control over the urge. The fact that I knew I was not supposed to move made it that much worse. Compounded by the fact that sitting for such a long time became uncomfortable very quickly, I began to develop a dread for story time. It was a shame, too, because it started out being one of my very favorite activities. I spent most of my time concentrating on trying not to move instead of concentrating on the story itself!

Everything was regimented and scheduled – not at all how learning actually takes place. We were required to walk everywhere in single file lines in utter silence. This seemed demeaning and very distressing to me, and I considered calling it quits when I saw it for the first time.

The bright spot in my day was the time we spent outdoors. I overheard one of the workers say that they were required to take us outside every day for a certain number of minutes. I had no idea who made this a requirement, but I was profoundly grateful to them for this reprieve. The playground was wonderful! There we were permitted to run and play at will, exercising our muscles and drawing the fresh air deep into our lungs. Every cell in my small frame felt oxygenated and energized, and we reveled in the freedom we found there.

Now they say for us to take a nap? Okay, let me see if I've got this straight: We eat cardboard on command, pretend we don't know the difference between a round and a square object, don't help others, sit and sleep on command, march in silent lines, and make strange noises. How does anyone survive this?

I heard the thought-words of one of the others, "We learn to code shift. That means that while we are among the ones who have forgotten, we pretend to be like them. We can be ourselves only when in the company of others who hear the thought-words and remember. Another important thing is that we must learn to talk the garble out loud. If we fail to do that, they will alter our brains with substances that make us forget."

That all sounded pretty scary and was not at all what I was expecting. I really thought it would be much easier this time around. I thought that they knew we were coming. I felt my sadness somehow turn into garble. I buried my head in my arm, trying to stop a strange physical reaction to my distress. I realized with great embarrassment that there were tears streaming down my face.

Oh, this is so humiliating! Please don't look at me, Ms. Pretty Eyes! I hope Lainy is still in the place of forgotten memories.

Thankfully, I heard the thought-words again. "This is all just part of the experience you agreed to have. Crying is what humans do when they are upset."

My distress was perfectly understandable. Forced feedings and blind obedience were difficult for me. I began to feel a little better when Ms. Pretty Eyes gently washed my face and took me to a blanket in the corner. I lay down, and she patted my back until I dozed off to sleep, still wondering what I had gotten myself into, but grateful, so grateful, that she was there.

Chapter 5

I was miserable. My stomach and head hurt, and I was afraid I was going to throw up any minute. I just let my head fall back on the car seat and looked at Mom's worried face in the rear-view mirror. I could still taste the chemicals from the cheese cardboard and wondered if that could be what was making me sick. The fact that I had been tortured all day with garble and schedules probably wasn't helping matters any.

When we arrived home, Mom got me out of the car seat just in time for everything I had eaten to come back up. Mom took one look at it and exclaimed in horror, "Oh, my goodness!! What did they feed you?"

I wanted to answer, but my mind was clouded with the events of the day and the chemicals to which my body was not accustomed. Mom took me into the house and went about the business of cleaning up the mess I had made. When she was finished, I just watched her from the sofa as she picked up the phone. My mind was not telling me who she was calling, and at the moment I was too sick to care. Usually I knew as soon as she reached for the phone.

Her voice sounded far away through the cloud of nausea. It was Aunt Sara on the line. I wasn't surprised because Aunt Sara always knew the right thing to do. Soon she was there beside me, putting down her basket and taking a look at me. I opened my eyes, and she knew at once what the problem was.

"Marissa, he has been poisoned."

Mom went kind of nuts for a minute until Sara stared her into calm as only Aunt Sara can. "This child has never been served fake food with additives and chemicals. Everything he has eaten his entire life has been clean and natural. We have grown our own food and have bought organic food items, all from trusted sources. From the smell of him he took in a lot of toxins today. I can even smell the chemicals from across the room. You are going to have to protect him and send his own food or this will happen until his system gets immune to the chemicals because he will be full of them."

Mom was ready to quit work and take me out of daycare, but Aunt Sara stopped her. "He must learn to be around other children," she said, "but you will have to protect him."

As she spoke she was searching through her basket. With a satisfied nod, she pulled out two small glass vials. One contained some kind of oil. In the other was a brown substance I didn't recognize. She directed Mom to put seven drops of the oil in the laundry detergent, all the body products in the house, and on my shoes. She rubbed some under my nose. It burned a little, but I still did not care enough to move. Then she gathered me up and took me outside for a walk. At first all I could do was sit on the ground. She sat with me, looking off into the distance, until I began to wake up. I still felt groggy, and all I really wanted to do was cry.

We walked around for what seemed like a long time. By the time I got back to the house I felt better. Sara told Mom what to say to help the staff at the daycare understand that I should eat only what she sent for me. She said something about "allergies." That night I did not hear my friends, and I could not see them either.

Myka watched with sadness as his friend suffered through toxic overload. He and the others were worried that this might change him and that he might not be able to hear or see them anymore. They had seen it happen many times in the past. The conscious pollution of a food supply stifled knowing and remembering. Surely now those in charge would stop it since they knew it was harmful. Surely they would see that money in the bank was not worth the loss of the voice within.

I fell into a fitful sleep. Nothing mom or dad did was right. They could not comfort me. Everything hurt, and I was lonely.

The next morning Mom woke me the same way she always did, with a song from her childhood. I loved to hear her sing, although Aunt Lyndee often teased her about it, calling for Stephanie to come save the song before it was too late. Her morning song was about a yellow bird, and I found it to be a happy, gentle way to greet each new day. Today, however, I was having a difficult time. Usually I jumped up, ready to see what the day would bring. Today I was sore all over, and I wondered if I were sick. I had not been sick very much and didn't really remember what it felt like. Mom was commenting on the darkness around my eyes. Maybe that was why I couldn't see very well – because there was something dark on my eyes.

Mom decided to stay at home with me and called to let the director of the daycare know that I would not be there that day. She gave me some tea which Aunt Sara had made the night before and put me back to bed. Aunt Sara knew how to make all different kinds of teas, and though they didn't always taste good, they always made me feel better.

I slept soundly for a long time, and when I awoke I felt better. My friends had been talking to me in my dreams. They told me that the food I had eaten at daycare had made me sick and that I had not been able to hear them. I knew it tasted bad. Mom heard me talking and came to get me. We had a long afternoon of just playing by ourselves. It was nice.

I was hearing my friends play, too, and it made me excited. The Little People who ran around at our house were a mischievous bunch who sometimes got me into trouble. They would knock things down and run from room to room. Mom thought I was the one doing it much of the time. They did not like it when Mom cleaned up everything so I tried to always leave some of my snacks out for them. They generally behaved better when I remembered to leave food for them.

The Little People told me that they did not let many adults see them. They would help sad or lost children without hesitation, but not adults. They said that unless somebody could see or hear them, it was not safe to make themselves known. Most of the time they stayed on top of the house, but today they were playing in my closet.

The next day I was well enough to return to daycare. Mom took along a bag she had packed for me. She told the teachers that I had had an "allergic reaction" to the food and that I must eat only what she brought for me. One teacher walked off when Mom was talking and rolled her eyes. Ms. Pretty Eyes came over, however, smiling and sending us thought-words, telling us she understood.

I saw Lainy, but she still did not know me. I wondered if maybe she had been having allergies, too. I decided that must be what was wrong. Maybe she had taken in so many chemicals that they had dulled her senses and stifled her awareness. It was a scary thought, but one I had to consider.

Playtime came and this time I sat on the floor waiting for the adults to tell me what to do next. One of them handed me a toy and moved me to the table. It had a box of what looked like squiggles and shapes. One of the others was ready to help. "Just take them out of the box and put them on the table." That is what I did, and it pleased the teacher who was sitting there. I was distracted, though, by the teacher's thoughts. I wondered why she was thinking about another place when she was here and if she knew that she could be in both places at the same time. I decided I would tell her.

Here you go - this is how you do it. Maybe you could try looking at me? Here - I will show you again.

I realized fairly quickly that she was not doing anything but moving the squiggles around on the table. I reached over and moved some of them, too, thinking this would please her. Instead she shouted, "Sit down, Jack!" I was shocked because I was only imitating her. I was still trying to figure it out as I sank into my chair. She called another teacher over, and they began to talk about me, glancing my way at intervals and frowning. One of them called Mom.

I could tell when Mom got there because I could feel her. When she came in she looked over at me and smiled, then went off with the teacher. I felt her coming back to me not long afterwards, and she was not happy. She collected my things and we left. She called Dad as soon as we got in the car.

I did not go there again.

Chapter 6

I loved it when Aunt Sara came to stay with me. It was a good day when Mom decided that I was not to attend daycare anymore. After all that, Aunt Sara came to spend those days with me. She brought my cousins sometimes, but they ignored me most of the time. They thought that I was too little to play with them. They did not play like I did anyway, and all the Little People hid from them. I was happy that they spent almost all of their time watching the television or playing video games. The only time I was uncomfortable was when Uncle Alex came over. He always upset Aunt Sara, and that always upset me.

Aunt Sara sang, and sometimes when Aunt Stephanie came, they would sing together. It was a glorious sound because their voices blended perfectly. I knew the tunes that they sang because I remembered them from a long time ago when I was grown up before. Aunt Sara could cook as well as she sang, and she made everything from scratch. One of my favorite meals was one she prepared on special days. She would fix bean bread and hominy. I remembered this from when I was here before, too. Mom would come in smiling because she knew what was cooking. The two of them would sit around the table and talk after supper about the old ways and how their mothers cooked.

It seemed that everyone in my family remembered the old times when traditional food was cooked. Dad had learned to eat it, but neither he nor Mom would use the fat back grease on the bread like Aunt Sara did. Sara would sneak a little on my plate. It was salty and smooth. Mom and Dad insisted that olive oil was healthier, but they were never able to convince Aunt Sara.

When Aunt Sara was around, all my other relatives came to visit her. This meant that I got to see them, too, and hear their thought-words. They all seemed to know how to send them. Well – *almost* all of them. Aunt Sara said that some of the odd ones were not responsible for what they did because they were "not of right mind." I wasn't sure I knew what she meant by that, but it seemed strange that they would be here at all if they were "not of right mind." Couldn't they swap the wrong mind for one that worked better? I wondered if they had forgotten how. I could have told them how to do it if they had asked.

I was so happy and excited when we moved into the new house in the country. I was overjoyed that Russ had waited for me. I had not been able to find him when we lived in town, though I had looked every time we passed the outdoor runs at the local animal shelter. He had told me before I came that he would be a red dog. He almost left before I could find him, but then Dad found our new home - and there he was, waiting for me!

One day a lady came over to our new house and asked if she could go to the woman's hut. Aunt Sara told her to go ahead. I was curious about where she was going so I watched as she went down the hill toward the pond. I crept through the tall grass like a real Indian, keeping low to the ground. She walked confidently through the field like she knew exactly where she was going. But there was nothing there!

With a start I suddenly realized that she was no longer there. She had disappeared! I stood up then and walked toward the pond, worried that she might have fallen into a hole or something. Then, there it was – a cabin with a long porch and people everywhere. They saw me and waved me over with the greatest of enthusiasm. I knew these women, and they were thrilled to see me. My great, great grandmother told me that I could come there any time until I was a teenager. Then I would not be able to visit anymore because I was a boy this time. I played with the other children for a while, then went back to the house. Aunt Sara asked if I had had fun. I told her I had and that I wanted to go back. She told me to sit down for a story first.

She said that the cabin was a woman's house. It was a place where the women went once a month to rest and be away from the hard work of keeping a home. It was only seen by those who knew the old ways. She said that male children could go there until they became young men. Then they would not be able to see it anymore. She went on to say that the cabin was not okay with some people which is the reason it stayed hidden. "Folks have a tendency to destroy things they don't understand," she said quietly. There was sadness in her voice, and I placed my hand on hers to comfort her. I did not tell her that I already knew this.

I asked how the cabin appeared the way it did when I drew near. Aunt Sara explained that it was in another dimension, one that existed at the same time but was hidden from view unless you crossed the line or lived in both places at the same time. This was necessary for its protection, she said. I wondered if there were other places like that, and did not hesitate to ask. Aunt Sara always answered my questions. She never just waved me off like they so often had done at the daycare center.

"There are lots of places like that, Jack. And during this time in which we are living, the number is going to grow, and more people are going to be able to see them. Soon there will be no difference between those places and ours. The only difference now is that some can see and some cannot. All those things that you see out of the corner of your eye but don't see when you turn your head are there in those places. Up here at this old homestead, all the other places that live at the same time can safely open. They know we will not harm them and that we know how to keep things in balance.

This is what led your parents to this place. It makes it more homey, don't you think, to see all that used to be and still is? There have been those among our people who for years have been able to see all of it at the same time. Those are our Seers. Sometimes they have been called Medicine or Holy people, too. We have always had these people who guided us, even when they were kept secret, to make sure we did not do anything to upset the balance of the worlds.

Lately we have had others wanting to do things that would upset that balance. They see a little glimpse and think that they all of sudden know everything. Some have shouted immediately, 'Look what I discovered!' in search of fame or recognition. They are ignorant fools to think that there is anything here we don't know about already. Taking care of the land that we have been given has been and still is our sacred duty. We have not forgotten our instructions. Nothing is lost in our memory. Nothing is hidden from the Seers!"

Aunt Sara's voice had risen, and so had she. What started out as a story for me had turned into an impassioned speech to a group of people only she could see. I knew she had been very upset recently at the latest group of discovers. She spoke often with my mother of her hope that they would not do too much harm or mess with anything that was unfolding in what she called "divine time." When some people came over a few months ago, I thought she would be nice for a minute then send them on their way like she usually did. I asked her later why she didn't.

    Her answer was a surprise to me. She said that it was time to talk to these people and for all to share what they knew. So she had talked with them long enough to discover that what they wanted was recognition and to become rich and famous for their "discoveries" which they were eager to publicize. They did not care for the place they thought they had discovered, and they did not care about the balance. They did not respect those who had always cared for the Earth places, either. She reported this immediately to the other Elders and backed away from it. She said she had already gone through a similar experience and that it was not hers this time. To engage in all that again would take her away from what she was supposed to be doing right now. She hoped they would stop and go home, leaving the Earth issues to the Earth People who knew and had been keeping the balance through all of time.

    I left her lost in her own thoughts and went to set the table before Mom and Dad came home. We would sit and eat together and extend the invitation to whomever was visiting at the time. My family always prepared extra food no matter what we were having. I heard Dad say once that it was one of his favorite traditions. I asked Aunt Lyndee about it one time, and she said that "somebody might stop by hungry" and that it would be a disgrace not to feed them. It meant a lot of leftovers sometimes, but everything was used even if the extra ended up feeding the animals we raised.

Tonight at supper Mom and Aunt Sara talked at length about the recent discoveries. Then the conversation turned to finishing the garden. They were thinking about doing the New Year gathering the old way, during which folks came and stayed for a week or more. Our new year was in October, and at that time we began our Winter Giveaway. Traditionally Winter Giveaway was celebrated to make sure that all the people had what they needed to get through the winter. I loved the New Year because friends and relatives came from all over to spend time together and share the news like they did a long time ago. Back then, they also traded the things they had made and feasted the entire time. It was so much fun to get to play with all of my cousins. Many of them had shared other lives with me so we knew each other quite well.

I asked if I could help get ready for the gathering, and they both smiled and said that of course I could. They promised that they would let me know the specifics when the time drew nearer. I went to my room to finish my homework. Later I went to sleep dreaming of the cool and colorful autumn which was just around the corner.

This was a beautiful place to be.

Chapter 7

Starting school this year was much easier than it had been in the past. I found that the more time I spent in this body, the easier it was for me to manage my human experience. I was ten years old and back at the same country school I had attended the year before. The teachers were nice, and my old friends were there, too. Some of them were friends from other times. Some of the new ones were cool, too. Aunt Sara said that we were being drawn to this place and that was why so many remembered. Our little town had become a gathering place for healers, just as Aunt Sara said it would. Many of their children were in school with me, as were some children who were healers themselves.

Of course there were some who could not hear the thought-words and were always talking about hunting and fishing. They were our friends, too, though I was surprised to learn that they did not seem to know about the hunt prayers. They had been taught to be thankful, however, and I was pleased about that. I have to say that at first I was very upset by them until Dad told me that this was the only way many of them could eat. After that when I would hear them talk about it, I would concentrate on giving thanks that they were fed. Mom said that some of this was the balance for all the good things that were happening and that it was all right. Aunt Lyndee was like me, though. It upset us both terribly when we heard the desperate cries of the animals in the woods behind our house as they fled for their lives. We felt their pain when they were shot and drew their last breaths.

It was just as bad when I heard the trees cry out as they were cut. Most of those that grew in the deep woods knew that they would eventually be cut down. But sometimes there would be an old one that had planned to die of old age in the same spot it had lived for many years. That was really sad to me. I could still hear the sound of their cries as they were carried away by big trucks which rumbled past our house. Dad said that sometimes humans had to do that to eat, too. Times were hard, he said, and there were not enough jobs to support all the families in our community.

School this year was the same as usual – worksheets and standardized tests in every subject. We did have a new math teacher who was so pretty that none of us could concentrate in her class. She smiled all the time and the best part was that she heard and understood thought-words. I found that for the first time in my life, I had to guard my thoughts because when she smiled at me, I couldn't help thinking how pretty she was. Her class was full of kids like me. None of us talked much out loud, but we had the best time! That plus the fact that it was all material we had done before made math class a breeze.

I heard Lainy as soon as she entered the building. I could hardly contain myself when the counselor brought our new student to our classroom to introduce her. "She is not new to me!" I thought.

Even though I was certain that it was Lainy – there was no mistaking that - I was somewhat puzzled because she looked so different than I remembered from daycare. She had reddish brown hair now and was much darker skinned than I recalled. She caught my eye and smiled. It was my Lainy, all right, even if she looked a little different from the pale blonde girl of our daycare days.

I wanted to talk with her at recess, but the other girls crowded around her. They were doing stupid stuff like showing their nails to each other. I would have to wait to talk with her, and that made me a little impatient. Her thought-words assured me that we would most definitely talk later. Sure enough, that afternoon she made a beeline to sit next to me on the bus. We were giggling in our thoughts but quiet on the outside. I asked her why she looked so different now and why she did not recognize me at daycare. She said that she had not stayed with the family she had originally chosen. When I saw her in daycare it was not really her - she had gone back to become a part of another family, a family who really needed her. They were going to lose their daughter because her body was flawed, and she had something really important to do. That was when Lainy stepped in and took the job. She said brightly, "Now we can do what we came here to do!"

I sat back thinking that things were finally the way I thought they would be. Some of my friends throughout lives were here with me now, and that gave me a feeling of great contentment. My growling stomach reminded me, however, that not everyone here wanted to be my friend. Ricky was one such person. He made fun of me every day and encouraged others to join him. He kept taking my lunch and shoving me into the wall in the hallway when I least expected it. I did not understand why he was so mean because I knew that he was one of the ones who could remember. I was perplexed that he always seemed so angry and decided I needed to talk to Mom about it when I got home from school - after I got something to eat, of course.

I looked out the window, lost in thought after Lainy got off the bus. My mind opened as I relaxed and saw the other places that were showing up along the way. People from the past and the future were turning and waving to me through the window of the bus. Every day there were more of them. It was a good feeling to look out and see all their faces. My understanding of how these worlds appeared grew deeper all the time. Sometimes there were strange animals – animals I did not recognize. They looked like they might be a mix of worlds. They were usually gone in one blink, and I would feel around to see if anyone else saw them. Sometimes they did and sometimes not.

As I got off at my stop I saw that Mom was home today. Russ met me in the yard and raced me to the house. I burst in shouting, "Mom! Lainy is here now!"

Mom turned and smiled. "That is great news! I know you have missed her."

Mom was cool like that. She knew things and helped me with my life agreement. I did not have to explain myself to her because most of the time she already knew.

I opened the refrigerator and began eating anything I could get my hands on. I was ravenous! Mom watched me for a minute and asked why I was so hungry. I hesitated for only a moment before launching into the story of Ricky and my stolen lunches.

"The thing is, Mom, it feels like I know him from before and that we are supposed to be here. He is always doing stuff like tripping and shoving me. When he demands that I hand over my lunch, I always give it to him because I can feel that he is hungry. But no matter how much he eats, he is still hungry! Sometimes he throws the food I give him, and I don't understand why he does that when he is hungry. There are some other boys who laugh at whatever he does, but they can't hear the thought-words like Ricky can."

Mom was silent for a minute. Then she asked about Ricky's live at home. The only thing I knew was what his sister had told us. She said that her mom and dad had taken Ricky in after he was found wandering the streets one cold night. He was a little boy at the time and had been left by himself. They did not know how long he had been living in the streets when he was found. Her dad was a police officer so he took him home, and they eventually adopted him. She said he was mean at home, too, and that she wished they would send him back.

Mom said that was what was wrong with Ricky and that I could make him better. She explained that he was picking on me because he knew I could fix it and take away his pain. She reminded me that he had made an agreement, too, but that somewhere along the way it had either gotten distorted or he had forgotten part of it. Maybe he agreed to be thrown away or maybe he was part of his parents' agreement. She said it sounded like he was having trouble re-entering his life agreement and that it was making him mean.

Mom said that she would start sending extra food to school with me so that I could share it with Ricky. She said that I should try to send him thought-words telling him he was welcome here and that we would help him. I thought about this for a while and could see that he was hurting so I knew she was right. I decided to try to make him better and help him see where to go from here.

The next day at school Ricky did not even look my way. I kept sending him thought-words, but he ignored them. I could tell that he heard them, too, but he never responded. At least he was not picking on me anymore.

GY Brown and PH Jones

Chapter 8

Middle School! I just knew it was going to be great! Mom and Aunt Sara were excited, too, because all of us were sharing this experience together. It was the first year we were allowed to play in the band, and I was so looking forward to that. Making music with other kids sounded wonderful to me, especially since Aunt Stephanie was helping. At first she did not want to do it because she said that football games hurt her head. I think she just didn't like to be out in the cold, but I eventually talked her into it. She was so talented and was so much fun. All the kids liked her, and she loved music so much that it made all of us love it, too.

It had been a great summer. Mom had allowed me to help with some of the Sacred duties this year. I even got to help the Grandfather who came down for the men's ceremonies. I was almost a man myself by this time and could be taken seriously. What I had to say seemed to matter to people now, even those who were not a part of the awareness into which I was born. I had finally grown taller and was no longer the shortest boy in class. Mom even let me get my hair cut like the other guys this year. Since my body blended in, this allowed my mind to relax and see even more. Kids my age were comfortable with our gifts now and had even started relying on us to do what we did best.

The first day of school I ran excitedly to catch the bus, eyes wide with the anticipation of my first year at the new middle school. The first person I saw was Ricky. He typically made it a point to glare at me whenever anyone else was around, but this day he halfway smiled at me. Seeing this as great progress, I considered sitting next to him but abandoned the idea when he sent the thought-words, "Don't even think about it, kid."

As I passed by him, I surreptitiously dropped a sandwich bag filled with homemade cookies next to him in the bus seat. He loved Mom's oatmeal cookies, and she had told him that if he behaved, she would make them for him regularly. He never really agreed to this out loud, but he stopped picking on me. True to her word, Mom made cookies for him nearly every week, which I discreetly delivered as I went to my seat on the bus.

The face looking back at us in the rear-view mirror was unfamiliar to us. The new driver was an old man with a scraggly beard and wire glasses. He wore shoes with no socks, and I wondered if his feet were cold on this cool morning. He looked up at this and laughed, sending the thought-words that I need not worry about him. Another aware adult! This was going to be a fine year.

After we picked up all the children and were at the school waiting our turn to unload I noticed there were police officers walking around. I could not feel why they were there and wondered what they were doing. As I tapped into them I felt a bad thing – Fear. The bus driver got my attention and told me in thought-words to stop worrying - that he and his friends would take care of it. He let me know that my job was to enjoy school and continue to code shift so that I blended in with the others.

There were older teachers everywhere when we got off the bus. They were busy telling us to act unaware and keep moving. As I passed by one of the police officers, I noticed that he did not have on the same uniform that our resource officer usually wore. I could feel him staring at my back, and I winced in pain. Just then one of the coaches stepped up and put his hand on my shoulder, saying in a loud voice that it was good to see me back. He was older, too - a bow-legged, rough-looking man, and I decided that he must have been from the high school. I did not know him, yet he seemed to know me.

Once we were in the building we were herded into the Gym-a-cafe-a-torium as everyone called it. We packed in like sardines, and I could hear the thought-words from my friends as we all wondered what was going on. When everyone was inside, the principal walked to a podium on the stage and waited for us to settle down.

"Welcome, students, to the new school year. It is going to be a great year. I am Ms. Beardlaw, your new principal. We have several new faculty members this year, and I want to begin by introducing them at this time."

We all watched as the new teachers, bus drivers, and maintenance workers came to the stage to be introduced. It seemed odd, but I knew all of them. They could hear thought-words and let us know that they could understand us. Ms. Beardlaw continued talking in real words. "For the next few weeks, we will have some special observers at our school. They are from the Consolidated Nations. They have been impressed with the test scores and how healthy the students are here at our school. They will be interviewing some of you, and we will be sending messages to your parents about that soon. At this time I would like to welcome the Consolidated Nations Task Force and ask that they come to the stage."

I studied the sullen force as they resentfully came to the stage. Ms. Beardlaw looked nervous and led us in a weak round of applause. This was scary. These people clearly were not here because they liked us or wanted goodness to grow and healing to continue. They did not like it that there were so many kids like me in one area. I could hear the concern in the thought-words of the others, too.

We knew these people had bad intentions. We could feel it. And we did not know what to do. I had never met hostility like this before. I felt physically sick and noticed that many others looked pale and drawn. The bad intentions were literally making us sick!

Then we heard the adults telling us everything would be fine. They assured us that they would take care of everything. They had seen this before and explained how to block the bad intentions. They confirmed that these people were here to find out why there were so many children with the new gifts at our school.

We were allowed to leave at last and go to our classes. It was the normal organized chaos that happens at the beginning of every school year. The observers were lost in the crowd.

When I got home that night I told Mom and Dad about the observers. They already knew they were there and wanted to know how I felt about them. I told them that they did not want what was best for the universe and that they did not like us. They pretended to like us, but it was clear that they didn't. Mom looked over at Dad, but this time I could not read her thoughts. It looked like she was remembering something but it was not from her life this round. Dad said that he wanted to be present during any interviews they did with me and that I was to call him if they singled me out.

The observers stayed a couple of weeks and then they were suddenly gone. None of them ever talked to me or to my friends. I don't even remember when they left. One day we had a new bus driver who was young. During that same week, we had a lot of new people working at the school. The older ones were gone.

    I told mom about it and asked if she knew what was happening. She told me that there was a group of people who did not want us to heal the universe. They thought that we children had a conspiracy that would be harmful to the government. They had been told that there were so many of us in certain places that we could rise up against them. I still did not get it because I had never had any thoughts about harming anything or anybody. Once they found out that we were not a threat, she said, they left.

    I was very grateful to the adults who had protected us from harm. They had made a way for us to come here, and they were keeping us safe.

Chapter 9

The end of middle school was near at last. There had been times when I thought the day would never come. It was one of the hardest periods of my life. My body was changing rapidly but was not able to keep up with my mind. Most of the teachers were shallow and seemed interested only in where they would be going on their next cruise. The few who were aware made the experience bearable. One in particular was Ms. Jonstone. If it had not been for her, I don't think I would have survived. I began each day in her homeroom, and she always greeted me with a warm smile. She gave me the encouragement I needed to make it through the morning until I came back to her for math in the afternoon.

Ms. J had a variety of comfortable seating in her room which lowered the stress she called "math anxiety." I was nervous about prealgebra until I saw how homey and inviting her room looked. She even had a dog named Reals! I loved his name and thought it was a great name. Ms. J always said, "Keep it real," but she said he was actually named for the set of Real numbers. Reals was part of a program called "Teachers' Pets" which promoted the training and use of therapy animals in schools. Every class should have a Reals!

The upcoming summer was going to be one to remember. I had started preparing my body for the ceremony that would declare me a man in my culture. Aunt Sara had been working with me for Thirteen Moons – her way of saying one year. During this time I had deprived my body of physical nutrients to prepare for a long fast. It had been easy for me. To tell the truth, it was kind of nice to have a reason not to eat very much! Every New Moon I had cleansed in the old way, and every Full Moon I had fed the Ancestors. Every day in between I had learned the stories that our people had kept pure and true through many generations. Every night I had visited with my people in the sky. I was ready to grow up now and take the responsibility to which I had agreed.

During the last week of school we were bused over to the high school. We were supposed to get "oriented" to the place. There were so many of us who were aware now that we really did not need to see it, but we went along with it anyway. Going through the halls was weird. There were lots of seniors who had other things on their minds. Some of those things were good things – things that would help fulfill their life agreements. Some of the things, though, were not so good. Those people were lost and had no idea what to do.

It made me sad to think that they might not be looking forward to the rest of their days here. Their dull eyes and sulky attitudes showed how unhappy they were. As we walked among them on our visit, we projected hope and goodness to them. We sent universal love and healing their way. Some responded. The brightest spots for us were those who knew us already and sent thought-words that they would be with us when we came back in the fall.

The Art and Music wing was the best place of all. One of the art teachers was waiting by her door for us. She was sending thought-words to us before we even reached her, telling us that it was going to be fine. Ms. Danko was a beacon of light and goodness at the high school. She was living her agreement to the fullest. She told us that she had done this many times, and that high school was an important rite of passage in the human world.

Summer came, which meant that I had four weeks to complete my transformation into the young man my Ancestors expected me to be in this life. Aunt Sara asked the Grandfather to oversee my progress. The ceremony would open with a big feast, and three days after that, I would go to the mountain.

My parents were a little wary of the upcoming process. Mom did not say anything out loud, but she was not as comfortable with it as I would have thought she would be. Dad did not get it, but his respect for the traditions was strong enough for him to give his blessing and approval.

Each day for the past thirteen moons I had followed the path to the water and cleansed the old way. During these magical walks I had met many new beings. Many were of Native ancestry. Some were from my European Ancestry. There were others, too, and each of them was equally wise - and very pleased with the coming ritual. I not only remembered my instructions but I was also eager to carry them out, and this forged a bond with the universe. We were certain that all creation would be blessed by our remembrance and observance of the ritual honoring this change in life phases.

The feast was a grand affair. Relatives of all degrees were honored as they attended. The places set at the table for unseen guests were naturally respected as much as if a visible person would be sitting there. The honor plates were prepared first. They were laden with the best of everything at the table. Plates were set out in the wooded area also to honor those who did not want to join in the human aspect of the feast. As was our custom, the Elders were served first and the children last.

Many of my friends let their children go first at family gatherings. We would never do that. The Elders were closer to the other side and heard the voices of wisdom clearly. To do anything less than honor them for their place in life, especially at meal time, would be a disgrace to the family.

Most of the time children were allowed to run around and do whatever they wanted as long as they were not in any danger. However, Feast and meals times were respected. It was not that long ago that food was scarce, and we made sure that the children who served themselves knew to take only small servings of each dish. They could go back but they were not allowed to pile up their plates like children in other cultures do. They had not earned the right to the first choice like the Elders had.

Today was an exception to this rule because the feast was held to honor my becoming a man and to send me off on my Sacred journey. So I actually got to be first in line with the Elders all around me. It felt weird and good at the same time. While my place in line had slowly moved up through the years, I had never even seen the front of it before now. I was becoming a man, and this was just a sample of what was to come.

Another of our mealtime customs was that we never cleaned our plates. We always left food for the Ancestors who were not with us physically but who always took care of us. We would cut out the best portion of food on our plate and offer it to the ones who watched over us. In a world where people still placed emphasis on cleaning one's plate, we were considered odd. It was especially difficult when I spent the night with friends. I was always afraid their moms would not understand that what we did not eat was a gift to the Ancestors and was meant to honor them. To deprive ourselves of the best on our plate was an offering. It was one of the many things that we did every day to stay in touch with who we were, where we came from, and where we were going. It showed that we remembered and were thankful for everything, including the one who had prepared the food. We sent extra blessings to them for their hard work with prayers of thankfulness.

    I was happy when Aunt Sara said the time had come for us to tell people what we were doing. I was lucky because most of my friends had parents who were open minded and tolerant. One of the moms showed me a quilt her grandmother had made. She said that, though the quilt squares were all different, they came together in beauty to make the whole quilt. I really liked that image, and I never forgot that people who were different could come together to make something really beautiful.

    After the feast we had storytelling done in the old way. This was not simply reading old legends and stories out of books. This was the old way in which each person was honored for his life and the important points and events he had experienced. The stories of each Elder's life and accomplishments were told first. We told them in the same order as we stood in the serving line, from oldest to youngest. It would be near daylight before it would be my turn.

Chapter 10

My first Journey with the Ancestors of this life began like these journeys have begun since the beginning of our time. After much feasting and fellowship I was taken out just as Mother Earth was coming to life. The Holy Man who was overseeing this portion of my journey led the way to a preselected location which he had been preparing since the last moon. When we reached a seam in the landscape, he turned and motioned for me to cross.

As I stepped to the other side, I found myself in another world. I looked back across the divide and could barely see those with whom I had been standing just moments before. They appeared to be in a sort of haze as the other dimensions typically looked. I realized with great excitement that I had crossed over fully into the place that had only appeared to me at times. I could smell smoke, but it was different than the smell to which I was accustomed. It had a pleasant, clean smell - a mixture of herbs and food. I could hear voices and see structures in the distance that had not been there before. I continued on the path toward the sounds and saw the Holy Man waiting for me.

He motioned for me to follow. We walked in silence for a while until we came to a ridge overlooking a small valley. There he indicated that I was to sit on a blanket that had appeared on the ground. He proceeded to draw a circle in the earth around me with his walking stick. When he completed the task he chanted and spread herbs on the outside of the circle. He continued sprinkling herbs in ever widening circles. I recognized some of them as protection herbs, but I was not sure of the purpose of the others. As he continued to spread the herbs in a circular motion, he moved farther and farther away. I watched in amazement as this took him out over the valley as though he were walking on solid ground instead of air.

Gradually the Holy Man faded from view. I could see the layers of existence in circles all around me. They appeared like the rings of a rainbow. I knew they were in layers but could see each one distinctly. I began the chant I had been taught for this special occasion. As I rattled my antler rattle to the rhythm of the chant, the first ring of existence opened and engulfed me in a life from long ago. I did not recognize it, though it did seem vaguely familiar. The landscape was rocky with gnarled trees scattered across the hillside. The grassy cover on the dry Earth was scratchy and pierced my skin. Once again I heard voices and began walking in their direction. I wondered if I should mark my path somehow in order to find my way back to the place where the Holy Man had left me. I turned and saw that the cuts the grass had made on my feet were leaving a trail of blood. My feet had stopped stinging so I continued on my way.

Presently I came upon a small fire, carefully laid out with stones surrounding it. Four logs set on end formed a triangle which pointed toward the sky. I approached the fire and sat beside it to examine my feet. To my surprise, there were no open cuts anywhere, and I looked back at the blood trail in amazement. I lay down by the fire to rest and fell into a gentle sleep.

Soon I began to see people of all colors come to sit around the fire. They were laughing and sharing a fine time. A clear, transparent person came into the group and began telling us the stories of Creation. As the stories progressed, the speaker changed from male to female and back again many times. The voice, which also changed, said, "The Spirit is genderless." The being then began to change colors, beginning with very light colors and fading into darker ones, then coming back again to light. The being said, "The Spirit is colorless." I watched once more as the being changed from an infant to an old person and back again. This time it said, "The Spirit is ageless."

    I awoke feeling refreshed. Looking at the place I thought I had been I could no longer see my blood-marked trail. I looked across the fire and saw that the trail clearly led through it into the next circle. I rose and followed it to a large cave inside of which shone a beautiful light. The light from the cave beckoned me inside where I found warmth and the smells of home. Huge crystals hung low and produced beautiful pure tones, each one having its own unique sound.

    Soon I discovered that I could understand the story they were telling of the Earth, the Mother of Creation. I sat and listened in awe at the story of how beings were created from Earth Mother and how she gave life to all things. The crystals also told stories about the first man and the first woman and how they provided food and life for their children.

    After a time I heard the Holy Man calling to me. When I stepped outside the cave, I knew I had stepped into another sacred circle. I did not see the Holy Man but clearly saw my blood trail once again. It led to a large body of water - so large that I could not see to the other side. I followed the trail across the water, and soon a whirlpool began slowly turning around me. I was unafraid as it twirled and twisted higher and higher. Finally it merged with the sky so that there was no discernable difference between water and sky. As it moved around me, I was given the knowledge held by the water. I came to understand that this water was the same water which had always been - the same water that I drank at home. Each drop held the history and Knowing – each held the story of creation.

After the water came to the end of all that it had to say, the turning slowed and I was gently placed upon the wind. I floated to a place where I could see the worlds I knew from a great distance. It was as though all the worlds were in the same place. They gently moved in and out of each other spiraling with color, life and sound. The wind carried me to the center of the valley that stretched beyond the ridge where my journey began. Suspended above the valley, I could see in all directions. From this vantage point I discovered that my blood trail formed spokes in four directions. The realization that I was at the center of the Medicine Wheel brought me great comfort. I understood that we are all at the center of our own Medicine Wheels and that all of Creation is around us, in us, and through us. We are the thing that always is.

I opened my eyes again and saw the Holy Man sitting across the fire from me. We were on solid ground now, but I still felt the sensation of floating. I reached out and placed both hands on the solid earth in order to ground myself before speaking. I asked the Holy Man if I were finished with my journey and how long I had been gone.

"Do not cloud your mind with time or space," he answered. "You will know you have been gone long enough when it is finished." With those words he vanished, and I was left once more on the blanket in front of a small stick fire on a cold mountain ridge. I began to chant again and merged with the chant on the wind as it circled around me and echoed back.

I began to hear sounds around me like those made by wild animals. I could hear their growls and footsteps, and I could smell their individual odors as they crept closer to me. I felt afraid for the first time on my journey as it occurred to me that at any moment the animals could jump from the darkness and tear me to pieces. Just as panic was setting in, I heard the sound of my chant circle back around to my ears. Once again I joined in the chant that I had sent out into the universe only a thought ago. The faster I chanted, the further away the wild animals became, and I realized I was safe.

Night turned into day once more, and I found myself growing hungry. Weak and lightheaded, I thought that surely I had been without food for days. A buzzard flew low and was soon joined by his friends. The flap of their wings created hot waves of air around me. Their obnoxious cries hurt my ears and their stench was unbearable. As they circled overhead I wondered if they were waiting for me to die of hunger. I covered my head with the blanket, hoping they would go away. When there was silence, I removed the blanket to see a very large, very magnificent buzzard sitting across from me.

The large bird turned his head and began to communicate clearly. I was not afraid because my human mind thought that I was dreaming. He began by telling me of the important function that he and his kind perform on Earth. He explained that their role as scavengers was of great importance in maintaining the balance of nature so critical to all existence. When he had finished he handed me one of his feathers and told me to hang it above the entrance to my home. He explained that it would keep nasty things from entering in the same way that he kept nasty things under control in nature. I sensed the importance of his gift and bowed my head momentarily to examine the feather in my hand. When I raised my head to thank him, he was gone.

Chapter 11

Sleep claimed my body and mind, and when I opened my eyes again, I found the Holy Man standing next to a tree, watching me with a smile. "You have done very well, Nephew," he said. Expression of any kind was rare among our Elders. They had mastered the stoic face expected of them so to be greeted with such a pleased expression was a great reward.

All of my questions seemed to tumble out at once: "Did you hear all of the wild animals? Were they coming to get me? Did you see the blood trail? Did you see the buzzard?"

I paused to take a breath and look out into the vast space before us. I turned back to him, half expecting him to be gone, but he was still there, still smiling at me. He handed me a thermos of some kind of tea, cautioning me to take small sips. Next he rubbed oil on his palms and smoothed it on my face and hands. His hands were rough but gentle, and as he sat down, he said, "Now. Tell me everything. Start from the beginning."

I talked for what seemed like days. Several times I realized that I had fallen asleep, but when I awoke I simply picked up where I had left off. At the end of my story I slept for a long time, and when I awoke the Holy Man was kneeling at the fire. I shifted to get a better look at what was most certainly a sacred task. "Hungry?" he asked. I smiled to see that this sacred task involved beans and hominy. We ate the food from old dented tin plates. It was the best meal I ever ate.

After we had eaten and rested, the Holy Man decided that we should spend the night there since it was getting dark. He told me that my final ceremonies would take place when we joined the others. At that time, he said, he would announce my new name. He cautioned me to keep my sacred name secret and to only use my public name. My sacred name carried great honor and responsibility, but few would ever know it. I would likely keep it for the rest of this life, he told me, though I would probably outgrow my public name. "Get ready to join the others," he said. "There will be feasting, dancing, and games. You will also have the opportunity to share the story of your journey."

The trip home was exhausting and seemed to take forever. At times it seemed that we were not moving at all. When we finally arrived, I could hear laughing and talking and could smell the aroma of food cooking. I could see all my cousins running and playing, too. I was glad to be home, but my skin was so tender to the touch that all the hugs, though welcome, were very uncomfortable. Such a crowd of people proved to be too much for me, and I wondered how old I had become when I asked for quiet and for the children to stop running. Everyone looked at me oddly, and I realized that I had stepped back and sounded very much like Aunt Sara did at the end of long gathering weekends. Mom intervened and suggested that I go to my room and rest before the feast began.

In the stillness of my room I collapsed on the bed. It felt different somehow, and I wondered if I had been gone so long that Mom had gotten a new one. Just how long had I been gone, anyway? Dragging myself over to my desk, I turned on the computer and saw that it was Tuesday. I had left on Friday. I was surprised because I thought that I had been gone at least a week. It did not matter, I decided as I fell back into bed.

I awoke to a great deal of shushing from the hallway as Mom herded the children out to the festivities.

I really should get up and get out there. This whole thing is in my honor, after all, and everyone has worked so hard to make it happen.

I got up and stuck my head out the door to ask Mom if I had time for a shower. She smiled proudly and told me to take all the time I wanted. When I stepped into the shower, the force of the water caused more pain than I could bear. I turned down the flow until it became barely a trickle and realized that my physical sensitivities were greatly heightened. Instinctively I knew that I must get them under control before I joined the others. I gradually increased the water flow until I could tolerate the shower spray at normal flow. Awareness flooded in at this desensitization.

So this is how the world takes over our minds and knowings. It pecks at us slowly with just enough increase that we don't run for cover or hide behind our knowing. It sneaks in slowly, gradually desensitizing us to whatever they are pushing at the moment.

After my shower I went back into my room to get dressed. Mom and Aunt Sara had hung a new shirt on my doorknob, a gift for my coming of age. It was one of the traditional shirts worn by the men of my Native culture. I proudly put it on over my jeans and fastened the traditional woven belt around my waist. I liked the way it swished when I walked. I was standing at the full length mirror admiring my new clothes when I saw the reflection of something on my bed. I looked more closely and thought my eyes must be playing tricks on me.

Is that what I think it is? Surely it can't be...........

Slowly I turned from the mirror, barely breathing. There on my bed lay a single buzzard feather. I moved in reverence to pick it up and turned back toward the mirror. Holding it high, I announced to the universe, "I am Buzzard Talking!"

Chapter 12

Everything about that summer was great. It seemed much longer than four weeks. The first week was spent on my sacred journey. I stayed at home the next week recuperating, ruminating, and getting ready to go on vacation with Grandmother Gloria. I didn't spend much time with her, but this year she wanted to take me on a vacation. She had decided that we would go to the beach and to Disney World. Aunt Sara was not sure it was a good idea because of all the crowds we would encounter. She said places like that often caused sensory overload for people like me, and she worried that I might get sick or be unhappy. Mom told her that Gloria was, after all, my grandmother and that she deserved to spend some time with me, too.

Gloria did not have the same kind of depth that Mom's side of the family had. She did not have our vision, either. She attached importance only to things she could see. To her, going to Disney World with your grandson was what good grandparents did. It was what she felt was the important thing to do, and that had to be respected.

When the day came to leave, Dad packed my things in the car and drove us to the airport. As usual Gloria's husband had backed out of the trip so it would just be the two of us. When we arrived at the airport, Dad asked a porter to help us with our bags. I saw Dad tip him and asked how I was to do this. Dad explained the number part of it, but the whole tipping issue bothered me. Why did you have to hand these helpers small bills of money? Were they in that much need? And if so, why didn't others take better care of them?

We had to stand in a long line to get to the waiting area for our flight, and it was the oddest experience. People were busy doing all sorts of things while they stood in line, apparently to avoid making eye contact with one another. Many of them became quite agitated with the waiting itself. It was as if they needed a distraction so that they would not have to talk or interact with their fellow travelers. But weren't we all fellow travelers in our human experience? Didn't that make us all one?

I was getting more and more uncomfortable with the whole feel of the place and found myself gritting my teeth, which really hurt my jaw. Gloria, on the other hand, seemed oblivious to the emotion and heightened mental state of the people in the area. I tried to concentrate on not gritting my teeth when I realized that I was getting too warm and that my pulse was racing. I did not understand why my body was reacting in this way. Was I getting sick? Gloria turned to me and said that it was going to be all right. She thought that I was having anxiety problems because I had never flown. She patted my hand and attempted to reassure me, "Flying is easy and fun! You will enjoy it!"

Bless her heart! She has no clue how much I know about flying. I don't need a plane and a room full of angry people just to fly!

We reached the security area where we were asked to empty our bags and pockets. A strange man felt my forehead and asked if I were sick. I shook my head, but he did not believe me and told us to move out of line. Gloria was stricken. Her face turned red and tears of embarrassment shone in her eyes.

We were ushered down a cold hallway to a room with a metal table and chairs. The noise in the hall was excruciating, like someone was pounding both my ears with cupped hands over and over, faster and faster. Once we were in the room at the end of the hall, the pounding stopped and there was nothing when the door was closed. It was a strange silence that hurt my head in a different way. I wondered what kind of room this was that blocked off all sound, all life, all feelings. There were no thought-words at all. Even Gloria was silent.

After what seemed like an eternity, three men and a woman came in, all looking very serious. The man in the suit felt mean. He began talking, but his words were not what he was thinking. He asked Gloria what we were doing and why we were going to Florida. She spilled out our vacation plans with a shaky voice. He asked why she was so nervous. She tried to tell him in regular words that she was embarrassed because they had taken us out of line, and she was afraid we would miss our flight. He did not believe her. I wondered how he could not believe her when she only spoke the truth.

Gloria did not like lying. The one lie she kept had taken so much of her spirit that she would not dare hold another. The man in the suit separated us by telling one of the men and the woman to take Gloria into another room. She protested that she did not want to leave me, but they ignored her. Her distress upset me, but the most distressing part was that no one could hear any of my thought-words. I finally had the sense to answer their questions in regular words.

When I told them that Gloria was my grandmother, they all huffed, and I felt a different emotion – anger. How dare they not believe me! The man then turned to me and told me to take off my clothes. I froze. What was this? I studied the man for a few moments. He was not a nice person. He motioned for the other man to assist me in removing my clothes. I did not want either of them to touch me so I undressed myself. The other man went through the articles of clothing while the suit waved a wand all over my body. The wand hurt. It felt like millions of tiny needles as it passed over my skin, causing me to wince. When they finished, he told me to get dressed and left the room with all of our belongings except my clothes. They even took my shoes. I cried out for help from the Ancestors and my friends that were floating outside. I could barely hear them because they were so far away. The Knowing told me to take deep breaths and settle my mind. I began to breathe deeply and sent my mind home to check on Mom and Aunt Sara.

After a very long time a different man opened the door and told me I could leave. I stepped out into the terrible noise to see Gloria standing there with a tear-stained face. They escorted us out of the hallway and into the main building. One of them mechanically uttered the words, "Have a nice trip."

We had missed our flight, and Gloria collapsed in tears. People were avoiding looking at us, and I had no idea what to do. Just then Gloria's cell phone rang. It was Mom. I took the phone and told her all that had happened. She said she would have Dad turn around and assured me he had not gone far.

When Dad came back, I asked if we could just go home but Gloria would not hear of it. We were bumped to a different flight so we had to get back in another line where we tried to stuff our belongings back into our bags. This time the man in the suit was waiting for us near the humming machines. He motioned us to stand in the machine. The machine sent pin pricks through my body at lightning speed. I cried out and felt my knees give way. I reached out to steady myself on the side of the scanner. Alarms went off, and the people working the scanner shouted not to touch the sides. Finally the alarms stopped, and they motioned me through. Gloria followed without incident.

    I realized that in this area, too, there were no Spirits hovering or moving about. It seemed very odd to me also that there was no humming from the thought-words that normally would be going on in a crowd. I looked at the people and realized there were no Spirits near any of them. This frightened me very badly. I spotted Dad waiting on the other side of the machine. He was smiling but also seemed concerned.

    I turned to Gloria and begged her not to make me go. I was crying and unable to control myself any more. Dad could see my distress and began frantically waving his arms at an airline employee. Finally she went over to him, then came over and asked Gloria if everything was okay. I simply could not take any more and told Gloria again that I wanted to go home. She was so worn out by this time that she agreed. After much talking and explaining, the employee led us back to Dad.

    On the way home Gloria continued to sniff and sob while Dad continually reassured her. This left little time for him to console me, but I was just glad that I could see and hear again and that the Spirits were all around us once more.

Chapter 13

I was so relieved to be heading back home after the airport event. I felt like a child running home after falling off my bike. I only wanted to feel Mom's arms around me and Russ's wet kisses on my face. I wanted to be where there were no painful sounds, wands, scanners, or anger. I wanted to drink water that did not burn my mouth with chemicals. I rolled down the window and took in deep breaths, letting the clear air wash away the grime of the city. I planned to go to the creek as soon as we got home and let the water wash off the pollution of the place of anger and confusion.

I felt Gloria's disappointment even though I did not understand it. I squeezed her shoulder several times during the drive home, and she weakly patted my hand. My mind cleared enough to feel her and hear her thought-words. I was so sad to hear that she was fearful of going home. "He" was expecting her to be gone for a week, and she knew that she would walk into something that she did not want to see. I asked her if she would like to spend a few days with us on the farm. She thought for a minute and said that since she was already packed and had the time, she would like that. I laughed at Dad's raised eyebrow in the rear-view mirror. He was so funny sometimes, worrying about little things. I said out loud that Mom would be all right with it. Dad suggested that I call her and explain that our plans had changed.

I could hear the relief in Mom's voice, knowing that I was coming home. She did not mind that Gloria was coming, too. I don't think she would have minded if I had brought the whole airport back as long as I was safe. She said that she also had a surprise for me.

When we drove up Mom was on the porch waiting with the hug I was looking for. She stepped back and motioned behind me. Russ came trotting out of the barn toward me as fast as his old legs would carry him. Behind him came a ball of white fur jumping over him, running under him, and making it difficult for him to walk. He did not seem to mind.

So this is why you were gone for a few days! You went to get a friend.

Russ looked at the energetic ball of fur, then back at me with eyes full of wisdom. Words were not needed.

What's his name, Russ?

Old Russ looked at the puppy and told me in thought-words that he thought his name was Lavey. The pup would not be still long enough to communicate without panting so we got no input from him. I motioned for Gloria to sit on the ground beside me. She hesitated until I told her Russ would not bother her. She gingerly sat on the grass just as Lavey took a flying leap and, with much more force than I thought possible, knocked her completely over. At first she was horrified. And then – something wonderful happened. Grandmother Gloria started to laugh. It was a sound I had not heard in a very long time. And as Lavey jumped on her chest and began licking her face, she only laughed harder. Finally she sat up and gathered the puppy in her arms, holding him close as he covered her face with kisses.

I looked at my grandmother and realized that this was the first time I had ever seen her relax. It certainly was the first time I had ever seen any dirt on her! The little twig poking out of her perfectly coiffed hair made her look younger all of a sudden. I told her that, and as she smiled I thought how beautiful she was with smudges of dirt on her face.

Mom called to us from the porch to tell us that she had made tea. I asked if I could go to the creek first and take Gloria with me so we could wash the "city" off. Mom was bewildered at the scene before her but recovered to say that she was good with that. The look on Gloria's face was amusing to me. "Come on, Grandmother Gloria!" I coaxed. "It will be fun." I started to add, "You're already dirty!" but didn't want to push my luck.

Gloria reluctantly let me pull her up from the ground, and we walked to the creek together for the first time - with Lavey running in between our feet and old Russ trotting along behind. Once there I began taking my shoes and shirt off. One look told me that my grandmother had no idea what to do. "Take your shoes off and wade out here," I instructed as I made my way to the deepest part and lay down. At first she was concerned about her clothes getting wet. I told her that Mom would dry them and invited her to let the cool clean water wash away all the bad stuff from the city. I was pleased when she did just that. As she lay down on the rocky creek bed I caught a glimpse of what she must have looked like before life took its toll on her. In this moment she was remembering her life agreement and was not worrying about the physical realm. She closed her eyes, and I saw her childhood, the hopes and dreams she had, and the reason she was here. It was a beautiful thing to see my grandmother for the first time without the trappings that had made a false construct of her life.

The water began its work, washing away years of confusion, disappointment, and pain. The cool water brought a healthy, true color back to her face. The dark streaks from makeup were washed away, and her cheeks began to glow. I was a bit surprised, really, that she was allowing so much water on her face until I realized that she was preparing herself for a transformation into her truth. I slowly made my way back to the bank, careful not to disturb her process. I sat quietly and kept her thoughts safe as she allowed the old to be washed from her. I don't know how long she would have stayed there if Lavey had not decided she was a launching pad. When he jumped on her she squealed like a young girl and opened her eyes. Her laughter rang out across the pure water, and the tears that mixed with it were from the euphoria she felt at her own Spirit's re-entry into her life agreement. I went back to the middle of the creek to help her up and in thought-words she thanked me for the most beautiful moment in her recent memory. She remembered.

We laughed as the water dripped down our legs, tickling them as it went. I handed her shoes to her but she took them in her hands and said she would just carry them. It was funny to see her walk barefoot, probably for the first time ever. I told her that we could stop and put our shoes back on, but she insisted that she wanted to feel everything.

Mom was shocked when she saw Gloria come in the house looking more like a wet cat than the proper southern bell. We all laughed and hugged knowing that this special moment was one that would sustain Gloria through the rest of her life's journey. I felt a contentment knowing that I had fulfilled a part of what I had hoped to do in this life.

Mom asked what we would like to eat, and when I answered, "The usual," Gloria said she would have what I was having. Mom got out the peanut butter and homemade apple butter. Grandmother Gloria fixed her sandwich the same way I did, copying every move. When she took the first bite she closed her eyes as the salty peanut butter mingled its flavor with the spicy, sweet apple butter. She did not even notice when some escaped onto her chin. She opened her eyes with a faraway look and said that she had not tasted anything that good since she was a little girl. The simple sandwich triggered her memory, and she began to tell us about her life as a young girl in the Deep South.

"This takes me back to hot summer days when I was young. We had a farm, but it was not like this one. It was a big, commercial farm with lots of workers. We grew sugar cane and cotton. The corn and soybeans that my brother grows there now were unheard of back then. Cotton was still king, and sugar made it sweeter. My dad would not let the old way go and insisted that the fields grow the same things his grandfather and father had grown. The field hands were mostly migrant workers, but there was one family that stayed all year. When I was very young, I was allowed to play with their children. They had a lot of children, too, all about the same age as me. Their mother was always smiling and singing as she worked.

The children had to work, too - every day except Sunday. I could not wait to get home from church so I could hurry to their house. They would wait for me, and we would all run down to the pond together where we would splash and play, catch frogs, and chase each other. When we got hungry, we would run back to their house where their mother would have hoe cakes filled with jam or jelly. We would eat so fast our faces would be covered in the sticky goodness, giving us a reason to return to the pond to wash. We explored the farm inch by inch during those summers, making discoveries together as happy, carefree children.

When I got older, my parents did not want me to play with them anymore. They would tell me that it was not "ladylike" or "proper." I continued to sneak down to their house, though, and we would run as free as birds, hair and hands flying in the breeze that our speed created.

Then one year my parents sent me to a different school – a school where students had to stay during the week. My parents told me it was where "proper young southern ladies" went to school. I was very unhappy there and could not wait to get back home to the farm so that I could see my Sunday playmates. I thought the first week would never end and was so excited to see Josey, our hired man, waiting outside to take me home. I asked him about my friends and if they had had a good week. He just said, "Miss Gloria, you need to ask your mamma these things, not me." I remember thinking what an odd answer that was.

Saturday was the longest day ever. I thought it was odd that I did not see my friends anywhere. I looked out the windows hoping to catch a glimpse of them in the fields. On Sunday the church service went on and on, but finally we got back home and after the longest Sunday dinner in history, I went to join my friends. At the top of the hill I shouted, "I'm here! I'm here!" But there was no answer.

I ran all the way to the house where they lived, and no one was there. Even the chickens in the yard were gone. I held my hands beside my face, peering through the windows, and saw that there were no colorful quilts, no bright pans - no smiles or laughter, either. Stunned and confused, I sat down on the front steps longing to smell hoe cakes and hear the voices of my friends. But there was only silence.

It was a long while before I walked back to my house, still trying to understand what could have happened. When I reached the house, my mother was sitting in the parlor so I asked her what had happened to my friends. She answered, "You are a young lady now. It won't do for you to be running around like a ruffian."

I went back to school the next day feeling like a part of me had died. The week passed without my doing anything other than what I was told to do. No thought was required, only obedience. All I had to do was go where I was told and look pretty. So that is what I did. On Fridays I went home for the weekend with a broken spirit. Eventually I would not go home at all. Home was no longer there - just a house full of old pretenses that refused to move out of the way for the circle of love to grow."

A long silence followed as my mother and I absorbed the words we had just heard. Grandmother Gloria's healing had begun.

Chapter 14

Mom, Dad and Aunt Sara all tried to prepare me for high school. Dad had all kinds of manly advice about how to be a good sport and a gentleman. It was all good information, but I could tell he had forgotten how many lifetimes I had lived. I was centuries older than he was, but I did not tell him this out of respect.

Mom reminded me that hormones make people crazy and that they take the place of good sense in people changing from one stage of life to the next. She told me people in this stage most often acted out of frustration and that they used peer pressure as a tool to make others as miserable as they were.

Aunt Sara talked to me about how it was harder for people like me to be in groups of unpredictable people. High school was full of unpredictable people, she reminded me. What was fine one minute was a battle cry the next. She told me how to avoid the traps that would send my knowing into hiding. I was ready.

I got off the bus full of goodness and excitement and went to find my first class through the throng of people, all scrambling to find their places as well. A loud buzzing sound virtually drowned out all the other noises. It was more than the bad electric wiring in the building, more than the lights that needed to be replaced. It was more than the hundreds of computers. It was the sound of unattached Spirits. I was not prepared for this.

I looked around in the hallway and as far as I could see the Spirits of many of the students drifted about a foot above them. The others like me were the only ones whose Spirits rested firmly inside of them. I told myself to find the good in this new phenomenon. The good was I could physically see who was aware and who wasn't. I assumed this was what adults meant when they said that high school was like another planet. I was tempted to go outside and see if the people outside had the same problem, but knew I had better find my assigned class.

When I got there, I was relieved to see that the Spirits of the teacher and many of the students were right where they should be. Some students in the back of the room were disassociated from their Spirits, but most were intact. A few were still trying to decide and were comforted when I sent them thought-words explaining what was happening. I really tried to focus on what we were being told but my mind kept wondering about the way the Spirits were in this place. The humans were not in any obvious distress or nearing a change in existence. It was more like the Spirits wanted to get a better view or check out the options or something. It was like nothing I had ever seen. I jerked back into reality when I heard my name called and answered, "Here." The teacher had already moved on like he already knew that.

When he finished calling the names on the list, he turned to the board behind him. He sent thought-words to those of us who could hear them: "This is the first day of a very necessary social experience in your journey as a human. Always remember you are among the frightened Unaware who act negatively in Fear. There are just as many of them as there are of you. Take them gently by the heart into the future, removing fear as you lead."

His physical appearance belied his Spiritual Beauty. He was physically short, pale, and bent. The glow around him, though, was magnificent! He raised his hand to write on the board, and his hand glowed like the rest of him with the whirling colors of a healthy existence. He wrote "Mr. Handly" on the board in funny letters, then turned and began talking to all of us. "My name is Mr. Handly. I have been teaching history for 24 years. You will be with me for first period because I am your adviser. I will guide each of you as you create your own history through high school and will help you as you set out on your adult journey. I have four grown children of my own who stop by from time to time to visit. My wife and I have been married for 42 years. She teaches science at the elementary school. I will not have each of you announce yourselves because I know how uncomfortable that can be. In time you will volunteer your story."

As he came to give me the stack of papers everyone got at the first of the year, he sent thought-words that it was all good. I watched him as he passed out the papers and continued to talk. He placed his hand on the shoulder of each of the unaware students and just silently communicated with the rest of us. I was amazed that each one he touched on the shoulder slowly got their Spirits back inside them. He is a healer, too, I thought! I am very lucky to be here first. No matter what else happens, I know Mr. Handly will understand and help make things better.

After he finished passing out the papers, he went back to his desk and told us to use this time to fill them out. I watched in amazement as his mind drifted back to all of his former students. He remembered every one that had passed through the doors of his classroom. Something was different, though. His memories included students from a time much further back than 24 years. Some of his students wore turn-of-the-last-century clothing and carried lunch pails with cloth covers. He connected with me and sent me the answers.

"I have been a teacher and guide for many lifetimes now. I was to be here to help others like you to continue and keep the goodness moving forward. Your class will be the last for me because you are the generation that will make universal love the governing factor and change history. You will be the ones who will stop the killing of anything good and the overuse of resources. You will make balance the rule rather than the exception. History will no longer be tragic lessons repeated but never learned. I will finally be able to really retire! You and your generation will be ready to take over and let me rest!"

Mr. Handley called out several names and told us to come back at the end of the day with our schedules. He would help us change anything that needed to be changed. I looked around the room and saw that many of the other students could hear thought-words better than out loud words like me.

The bell rang and it was time to go to a different room. Once out in the hallway the mass chaos engulfed me again. This time there were fewer disassociated students and many more who could hear clearly and see further than before. I realized that even those who had a limited remembering still could hear and see the broader present and move forward.

The average persons, the ones in the majority, had become more aware in one lifetime. They had absorbed the Knowing of generations and now were the physical embodiment of the Knowing. There were a few, of course, who had chosen another destiny. I was glad they had because they reminded us that there was a difference between remembering and forgetting. They kept complacency before us so that we would not forget its danger.

The rest of the day was a blur. I watched as Mr. Handly and a few other teachers like him reset many disassociated Spirits. Those that did not reset wandered through high school like they wandered through life with very little awareness of anything other than the physical. They were easy to spot in a crowd. Even if you could not see the detached part of them, you could see the blank look in their eyes which all but shouted, "Nobody is home."

No wonder Mr. Handly is ready to retire! This is exhausting work that he and the others do. Their life agreements must have included this action to be able to do it so fluidly without collapsing on the spot.

I added my energy to the task, and he caught my eye through the crowd at lunch, thanking me for my contribution. "This is important work which has to be done. Every Spirit has the chance to remember. We offer them another chance. If they take it, wonderful. If they decline, it just is. We help them where they are, not where we want them to be."

I was thrilled with thoughts about the responsibilities described by my teacher and began planning his retirement gift at once. I would carve him something out of the wood left in our barn. The wood still talked of the past and held the laughter of the generations of children who had played there. It was a happy wood and would be just right for Mr. Handly.

Chapter 15

After telling Mom, Dad, and Aunt Sara about Mr. Handly, I told them that I wanted to start to work on a carving for him. I went out to the old barn and stood in the doorway for a while. There were old tools hanging about from the previous owners. Most were broken, but still they hung in places of honor. Many looked to still be in working order, just waiting for a calloused hand to put them to good use. I doubted Dad would ever use them. I pulled up an old milking stool and closed my eyes to listen to the old barn talk.

I soon realized that Lucas was near and told him to make himself comfortable while we listened to the story of the barn together.

The vision began in the woods around the property. A young man had ridden his horse to the creek for a drink of water, pausing for a moment to sit on a fallen log. He had finished building a house for his sweetheart and hoped to bring her there soon. He knew that he needed to get the barn built before winter to shelter the animals and farm equipment. While his horse drank, he carefully studied the trees around him. He mentally asked them how they would like to be part of the barn. As I watched him I knew I was seeing an earlier, more primitive form of thought-words. He did not hear their answers as he set about marking them. He could not hear their cries as he carved their outer bark with his knife.

A few days later he came back with friends to set up a saw mill. Soon they were ready to begin cutting down the trees. He and his friends were lucky they could not hear the cries of the trees. If they had they might never have slept again. They cut the trees then fed them through the mill to make lumber for the barn. By the time they were made into boards, the trees had fallen silent. Their fate was sealed, and they were resigned to becoming part of a building. The man and his friends loaded the boards onto a mule cart and transported them to the site of the new barn.

  The next day whole families arrived. The boards watched as the women set up tables and started fires under large pots. The men unpacked their tools while children played all around. When everyone had arrived, they were divided into teams to begin the construction of the barn. It was an ordinary enough barn raising except for the child sitting under a tree. The boards watched as this child fretted and drooled. Occasionally a woman would check on him and wipe his mouth. Though the child was unable to communicate with other humans, he could talk with the boards and all the other parts of creation. He told the boards that he was there to watch and to remember.

  The boards told us how each nail felt as it was driven into the wood. Lucas and I found ourselves being very glad we had never been a tree by the time they finished their story. They told how on occasion the young man would come into the barn in later years and drive another nail on which to hang a tool. It hurt less and less over time, and they told me that if I drove a nail now they would barely be able to feel it because they had grown so tough. I saw and heard the many animals that had been sheltered by the barn throughout the years along with the births and deaths that had passed through it. I saw also stolen kisses and hearts that had been broken there. The marks of many ended dreams and spilled tears were clear on the wall and floor in a hidden corner. In contrast the bright shining places where dreams were born and furniture made with loving hands still glowed with good energy. Here, once again, was the balance.

    I saw that the old stack of carving wood had in later years been the man's only friend. He would have traded every splinter of that wood for one visit from his children. I saw where his spirit moved out of his body, leaving an imprint of his sorrow on the spot where he drew his last breath. I walked over to the stack of wood and began sorting through the pieces. At first they were silent. But after I had moved the ones on top, I began to find a variety of partially finished items. Most were toys. As I picked up each one I could see the child for whom the old man was carving it - children he loved dearly and who must have been his grandchildren. Some of the toys even had names on them and were signed "Love, Pawpaw." I was saddened that these pieces had never made it to the children for whom they were intended.

    At the bottom of the pile, I found a rough ball of wood. It was different from the others in both color and texture. The other pieces of wood were easily recognizable - ash, birch, and maple. A few pieces had been black oak. This one was like no other wood there. As I held it, jerky images in black and white flashed by. I took the rough round of wood in my hands and sat down with it, willing it to continue telling me its story.

    The wood was part of the bottom of a boat which was sailing on a rough sea. A little boy who looked to be six or seven years old was in the boat, picking at a knothole on a plank. He was leaning against his mother who appeared to be gravely ill. For days the little boy picked at the knothole, finally working it loose. He began tossing the rough ball and catching it without ever making a sound. When he heard the door above him open, he would hide his treasure in his pocket.

One day the door opened and a man came down to the place where the boy sat with his mother and the others. The man went through the group of people in the bottom of the boat telling some to go up and out of the hold. The boy did not want to leave his mother, but the man snatched him and handed him to another man. That was the last time he saw his mother here. He clutched the knot of wood in his hand as he was roughly transported to a big farm by buggy. When he reached the farm, he was given to another family that already had several children. The parents took pity on him and shared what little they had with him. The only possession the boy had - his only connection to the past - was that knothole.

As the boy grew older he continued to keep the knothole safe in his pocket. One evening, exhausted from working in the fields, he did not notice that the piece of wood was missing. He searched and searched but never found its hiding place in the corner of the barn.

I told Lucas that I thought this was the perfect gift for Mr. Handly. I would not carve it or do anything to it. A piece of wood like this was a gift no one else would understand. I knew instinctively that Mr. Handly would be able to both see and hear the story and would know how to honor the piece of wood, the story, and the original keeper of the knothole.

It was almost dark before I left the barn. I told Mom and Dad at supper that night about the knothole and the story it had shared with us. They were not surprised and thought that it would be a meaningful gift for Mr. Handly.

The next day I took the knothole and gave it Mr. Handly. When he took it in his hands, he sat down and removed his glasses. He closed his eyes for a long time, then related more of the story to me in thought-words.

The little boy had been a happy boy with a mom and dad and two sisters. His dad had been a shoe cobbler in Europe. The little boy had a good life and there was always plenty of food in his warm home. One day his father did not come home. His mother looked for him all through the night to no avail, returning home the next morning, distraught and exhausted. Not long after her return a stranger knocked on their door with the news that his father had come across some very bad men who had killed him for the little bit of money he had in his pocket.

The boy's life was filled only with sadness after that. Strange men came and removed them from their home. His sisters were taken away, and he and his mother were thrown on a boat and sent far away. Mr. Handly looked up and explained that they had been sold into servitude to pay the debts left by his father. The family lost everything including their freedom. The boy's mother died on her way to this country. The little boy served by working on the farm where the knot was found. He would spend the rest of his life there but would never know freedom because the cost for both him and his mother was too great.

"This is a knot from Linden wood. It does not grow in this part of the world," he said softly.

I asked Mr. Handly how it was possible for him to see the whole story in such exact detail. He looked at me with tear-filled eyes and sent pictures with his thought-words. My own eyes widened and filled with tears as I saw that Mr. Handly was that little boy in another life. I was stunned and did not know what to say. I could feel the same pain in his past life that I felt in Aunt Sara's. He knew my thoughts and said, "Many people who came here did not want to do so. They were forced to come and work for the same people who seized the land from those who were already here. Once they made their life agreements, Jack, they had no choice."

Not even thought-words were necessary for Mr. Handly to express his deep gratitude. I knew how much the gift meant to him by the tears in his eyes and the way he carefully cradled the knothole. The simple ball of wood had made its way across many years and an ocean to rest once again like a treasure in his hands.

Chapter 16

Through the fog of my dream, I could hear the sound of voices in the distance. As I focused on their serious tone, I saw the source of their concern. Not far from where I stood was a group of people poised to send a projectile into Grandmother Moon. She was in great distress and was already feeling the pain of her skin being ripped away as the missile entered her body. Then, just like that - it happened. Bits exploded from her breast, and she cried aloud in anguish. Her cries were not just for the pain she felt in that moment, however. They were also for the things to come. She lost her place in the universe for only a few seconds, but it was enough to disrupt the natural order and balance that was hers to maintain.

My vision shifted to the scene on Earth. There was chaos everywhere. Thousands of Spirits floated about, trying to make sense of what had just happened. Government officials met behind closed doors, scientists pored over charts and talked in hushed tones, and children peered through half closed blinds at deserted streets. Schools were empty and businesses were closed. A thick blanket of Fear lay over the Earth Plane.

I looked to my left and saw that Myka and the others were dimmer than usual. They were much more concentrated and were guarding their energy. I heard their concerns as they felt the shift in the thin fabric that separated them from the rest of creation.

I focused on my home and family to make sure they were all right. Dad had not gone to work and was talking with Mom and Aunt Sara in the kitchen.............

I woke from my dream in my warm bed, smelling fresh coffee and sweet bread. Aunt Sara made Stephanie's favorite - sweet bread - anytime she came to visit. My mind briefly revisited last night's high school graduation ceremony and the family dinner that had followed. All the parties and celebrations my friends were having did not interest me. Getting wasted was not something I wanted to do when there was so much for which to be thankful. I was much happier having a small dinner celebration with good food and people who sincerely loved each other. It had been nice to have my aunts there, and I was so glad they had stayed over. Especially now.

I began stretching my body and warming up my muscles before leaving my bed. I felt around in vision to see if anyone else knew what had happened. Since everything that happened here had already happened, there was little that could be done to stop the events I had seen. The thought-words from the other room told me that the others knew so I got dressed and went to comfort them. As I passed by my window I saw that there was a different hue to the air outside, a bluish cast in place of the normal clear or golden tint of the morning.

Mom, Dad, and Aunt Sara turned to look at me as I entered the room, concern written all over their faces. "Don't worry," I said. "The worst is over. Now we have to help where we can and comfort those who are frightened. There will be another wave of sorrow to enter the universe when daylight shines on the rest of the world. We must prepare for that. We have to be ready to send out love to balance the sorrow."

Dad looked at me like he did so often these days. He still did not totally get it although he really did try. "This is serious, Jack. We can't go anywhere to comfort anyone! The National Guard is blocking all the roads, and businesses and schools have been ordered to close. They even told me not to come to the hospital! They said they would send the Guard for me when they needed me."

I walked over to my father and put my arm around his shoulders. I wondered when he had gotten so small and lightly squeezed him in reassurance. "It will be all right dad. It has all already happened. We just need to make sure that we don't do anything to upset the recovery and add to the Fear."

Looking up at me, Dad shook his head. "I hope so, Jack. I really hope so."

Dad still had a hard time comprehending the existence I shared with Creation. It was difficult for him to see past the physical. He supported me and my visions but really did not understand. At times like this he was even more skeptical. The physical was so present in tragedy it was hard not to be.

Mom had gone into the family room where she had turned on the television. Images of chaos and destruction filled the screen. Fires, giant holes in the Earth, water covered cities, buildings in crumbled heaps, people screaming and bleeding in every corner of the globe – it was all unfolding in front of us.

The power flickered and the phones rang those half rings they do when something is wrong with the power. Overhead we could hear the sound of military aircrafts racing by. Normally we never heard aircraft since we lived on the edge of a protected natural area. I liked it that way because they really hurt my ears and the vibrations shook my insides. During disaster, apparently, restricted air space was lifted.

Aunt Sara had gone to build a fire in the old wood stove. She already knew we would be losing power shortly. The solar generators would have to be used sparingly to keep the water flowing and the refrigerator running. She would heat and cook the old way. I went to carry in wood for her so that I could be in her calm presence. She smiled at me and sent her thanks and love. Her thought-words asked what had happened.

I told her that someone had sent a rocket to the moon to take her apart. They had blasted her so hard she had tipped and spun in a way that made her dizzy. She had even bumped into some of the stars as she reeled from the blow. Sara nodded and closed her eyes to offer prayer for Grandmother Moon.

The blast set off a chain reaction of earthquakes, tsunamis, typhoons and other disruptions on Earth. Was there no sense in humans? Grandmother Moon controlled so many important things. I did not know how to make this one right. I only hoped my friends did. The thought-words sent out across the universe told us that we would get together shortly and help with the recovery. We were first to help our physical families come together in a stable environment for the important work ahead.

Aunt Sara said that we must set to work so that darkness would not find us unprepared. The old oil lanterns were cleaned and refilled. The iron pots and pans were brought up from the basement, and Mom and Aunt Sara made sure things were where they could easily find them.

Lyndee stumbled in, following the smell of coffee with half closed eyes. I started to talk to her but she held up a finger in the "not now" motion I knew so well. She was not fit to talk to before she had drunk her coffee. She had always been that way. After her first few sips she looked at me and said, "Go bother Aunt Stephie." I bristled a bit and reminded her that I was no longer five years old. She just looked at me over her coffee cup and winked. Mom brought us back to the present by turning up the volume on the TV.

Aunt Stephanie padded softly into the kitchen, smiling a sleepy smile to everyone present and to the universe in general. She always got up smiling. She went to Aunt Sara and gave her a warm hug when she smelled the sweet bread. Next she came to me and buried her head in my shoulder, asking in a sleepy voice what I wanted her to do. She was one of the kindest Spirits I had ever met and was always ready to help even when she had no idea what had happened. She just knew that right now something needed her attention.

Dad had taken up his post in the living room where he would spend most of his energy watching out the window. Part of him hoped the hospital would send someone after him so that he could start doing something to help. Part of him did not want to leave us. As night fell he was still there, looking toward town.

After everyone had eaten breakfast, I asked Stephanie if she would play the piano. She smiled and went over to the old piano, pausing before it in respect. I walked back to my room to lie down and begin my work. It was comforting to hear the soft notes lovingly played in the other room as I traveled to the place of Knowing. Once fully there I found that others like me were already working to restore peace. In some places the balance was greatly disturbed, and we moved on to the ones which could be righted the most easily. We knew that the more that were righted the easier it would be to balance the worst places. We were doing what we did best even though we were so very sad that humans had created this by tampering with things they did not understand.

Chapter 17

I could not believe my eyes. Across the room from where I stood was the most beautiful creature I had ever seen. She was talking with a group of friends at the college mixer sponsored by our student government. My roommate Hunter had insisted that I come, practically forcing me by saying that it was here that I would meet the girl of my dreams. I typically avoided all types of social functions, but he eventually wore me down, and I agreed to put in an appearance. "Just to shut you up," I told him. He had been my roommate since freshman year and was very intuitive and aware, but I suspected that the real reason he wanted me to come was that he just didn't want to come by himself.

But standing there now – looking at this girl – I wasn't so sure anymore. What if he was right? My heart raced, and my knees trembled. What was this powerful thing that was taking over my body, mind, and Spirit? She turned and smiled at me, closing the distance in the large room full of people. Suddenly it was only the two of us, held apart from the rest in a prism suspended above all that was solid.

She spoke, breaking the spell. "Don't I know you?" she asked.

I knew I was supposed to answer but could not speak. At least I thought that I couldn't until I heard my answer, "Yes, you do know me. I am the man with whom you are going to spend the rest of your Earth walk."

Her eyes widened, and I wanted to disappear.

What part of me would say something like that? What is wrong with me?

Sweat beaded up on my forehead, and my mouth went dry as I heard her answer, as if from far away, "Is that so, now? Do you think I should at least know the name of the man who has decided to intrude so completely upon my life agreement?"

Hunter appeared and rescued me just in time. "I see you two have already met! I knew we would be sharing this experience together!" He was like a big Lab puppy, so happy and proud of himself.

The beautiful girl informed Hunter that we had not met at all - that I had only claimed her like a caveman declaring he had found his woman. Hunter laughed and slapped me on the back. "Jack, this is Sam. Sam, this is Jack."

I extended my hand. "Sam?" I asked.

"Short for Samantha. Is Jack short for Jackson?" I nodded mutely.

"Very nice to meet you – I think," she said. As she returned to her friends, she called back over her shoulder, "See you later!"

The Lab puppy was grinning from ear to ear. "See what I meant when I said that your wife was going to be here? Isn't she perfect for you? I have already seen your lives together, buddy. She has, too, though she might not remember it at the moment."

I grinned in spite of myself and told him that might not happen since I had delivered the worst opening line in the history of all lines. I felt like I had run a mile uphill and was pretty sure I was going to be sick. Hunter laughed again and said, "When the love bug bites..."

That was lame, even for Hunter, I thought, who was always quoting some silly phrase from the past. But I had to admit he had a point. I did feel like I had contracted some sort of bug.

The next afternoon as I was sitting at the coffee shop working at my computer, all I could do was think about her. I tried to concentrate on the paper that was due the following day, but my mind kept seeing her, feeling the colors of our moment, hearing her voice. I looked up to clear my head and saw that she was there, walking toward me. I scrambled to my feet and pulled out a chair for her, hoping to convince her that I was not the Neanderthal she had first met. She was impressed. "So you are a gentleman after all, I see. Not many of those around."

I was lost in her smile all over again. I pleaded for the Knowing not to let me make a total fool of myself – again - and asked what she would like to drink. She opened her satchel and pulled out her own thermos, pouring herself a cup of tea. "I have my own blend from home. I like it better than anything served here and it keeps me close in memory to my home and family."

Life moved on from there as though we were old friends who had fallen in love. That was true, too, since we had shared many other lives together. This was one of those relationships that truly was just meant to be. I knew when I saw her that our remaining time here would be spent together. She told me later that she knew it, too.

We had to have more than one wedding ceremony because Dad and Sam's family were traditional in the

Western way, and the rest of my family was traditional in the Native way. Aunt Sara would perform the traditional Native ceremony and blessings, and it was the one that mattered most to me. It was not like other ceremonies that were contract oriented. Written contracts were easily broken. In the Native way it was not so easy. The promises we made were also agreements with Creation and all the parts of the universe. Our promises were sealed when an earthen vessel was shattered and given back to the Earth. The only way that promise could be undone was if the Earth returned all the fragments of the vessel, and the vase could be made whole again.

    The day came for the traditional ceremony. Aunt Sara looked beautiful in her ceremonial attire. The power of generations of Earth women glowed all around her. She was the embodiment of all who came before her. She supervised the preparations and blessed the area for the required seven days. We were so happy that she was able to do it. She was getting older now and was not as energetic as she had once been, though she still surprised me with all she could accomplish in a day. The aroma of our sacred herbs filled the air, and ancestors from further back than I remembered hovered nearby. The universe seemed to be filled with the joy of our laughter.

    Sam's family was not sure about the lack of structure, but they tried to understand. They accepted my family as a loveable oddity. They truly loved me and were genuinely happy that we were going to share life. The young girls got Sam ready with much giggling and excitement. They draped the blue blanket around her shoulders while Aunt Stephanie kept a watchful eye to make sure that nothing was out of place. When she picked up her flute we knew it would soon be time to enter the ceremonial area.

Dad and Mom straightened my clothing and made sure that my offering was complete. Then Mom and Lyndee placed the blue blanket around my shoulders. I saw Mom catch her breath and touch her cheek as Lucas kissed her and gave me the greatest blessing he could give: "May your life be as full of love and laughter as mine was with Naomi." I knew that their love was one of the greatest of all time and wanted Sam and me to have the same kind of devotion for each another.

Mom joined the other members of our Clan and led the procession to the arbor. We waited for Sam and her family to join us. All of creation seemed to bow to Sam's beauty as she walked to the arbor. Silence followed as Aunt Sara walked regally to take her place. She began with a prayer and stated the purpose of the ceremony. Then she asked that our families bring Sam and me to stand before her.

Sam's family still looked a little dubious but remained respectful of our way. Aunt Sara asked for our promises, and when we had spoken them, we handed each other the traditional baskets representing our promises. We then presented the baskets to our families, symbolizing the promises we were making to them. Sara held the wedding vase high for all to see as she explained its significance, and we drank from the vase before turning to face the crowd. Our families placed the bond of the white blanket around us and walked with us to the creek bank. There I shattered the vase and allowed the pieces to tumble into the water, returning it to the Earth from which it was created.

A glorious feast followed where we enjoyed our

families and our new status as a couple. Many well wishes were given throughout the night, mostly for healthy children and a long life together. I had a feeling that this was just one of many lives I would share with Sam.

    We slept most of the next day and prepared for the other ceremony. This ceremony was required not only for legal reasons but also for the comfort and happiness of Sam's grandmother. We wanted the members of her family to feel good about our earthly union, too. Looking back on it later, we realized that our wedding was everything we hoped it would be - a beautiful example of how people of different paths can respect and honor one another's customs and traditions and move forward together in perfect acceptance and love.

Chapter 18

Sam and I settled into our life together without fanfare. We had already begun building our cabin down by the pond where Aunt Sara's had been planned. We never got around to building hers because she moved in with us after Uncle Henry crossed to the other side. We kept Sam's apartment in the city to have a place to stay when we were working there. I had difficulty handling my time in the city and had to work from home most of the time.

Building our home was an enjoyable task. We used only renewable materials and were determined to keep it modest. Neither of us used more than we needed, and we always considered the effect of our actions on nature and its impact on future generations. Aunt Sara gave us most of the furnishings she had in storage so there was not much left to buy or make. We used solar power with very little current inside. It gave me great peace to be in a place where there were few frequencies because we were much healthier if we were away from power lines and chemicals.

My work as a historian led to a career as a writer so it was easy for me to work from home and only go to the office a couple of days a week. Sam's job as a transportation engineer required her to go into the city more often. We tried to coordinate our schedules so that we were both there at the same time to reduce the amount of travel.

One day when I was working from home, I decided to take a break and go down to the pond. It was an early summer day, and the reflection of the sun on the water made me very sleepy. I lay down in the soft grass to rest for just a minute.

My dream world opened up in a different place. It was filled with crystalline hues and low tones. I went with it and began to explore these new surroundings. The clear colors gently swirled as I moved through them. I could hear the voices of children laughing and talking, and when I turned toward them I saw many young spirits watching the people on Earth and other planets. They moved into groups as they chose a planet. I realized that they were getting ready to enter life and watched as they selected the place where they would spend their next lifetimes. I remembered this process well and was fascinated to see it as an observer.

One of the Spirits turned and began inquiring about my views on life. I realized with amusement that I was being interviewed by my potential child! The questions were good ones, mostly about my world view and the things I had learned during my time on Earth. The final questions were, "Do you think that the humans have learned anything? Is there hope for a peaceful existence in that place?" I thought for a moment about all the things I had seen and how much progress had been made before answering.

"Yes, there is hope. The goodness that began decades ago has continued to grow. The people have accepted me and my mission completely. Persecution of those who are different is virtually absent now in the human psyche. The ability to discern reality has opened up among the masses. Most importantly, they are on the cusp of realizing critical mass awareness." The Spirit asking the questions was pleased with my answers. The interview ended with a playful, "See you soon, Dad".

My eyes flew open, and I awoke with great excitement. I was about to be a father!
I raced back to the car, jumped in, and demanded it get Sam for me. I waited impatiently to hear her voice, so excited I could hardly contain myself. I even found myself looking at the time, and I never looked at the time! Man made constructs were alien concepts to me and always had been. I was grateful that Mom had taught me to use notes and alarms to be where I was supposed to be at any given time. I was never late, but it was not because I actually knew what time or even what day it was.
Finally I heard Sam's voice. "What's up?" I began talking so fast she could not understand a word. With great effort, I forced myself to slow down and concentrate on my communication. "We're having a baby!"
A long silence followed, then Sam spoke. "I will be home in a while, and we will talk. In the meantime - are you alone?"

Great! She thinks I am off in another reality again. How can she not see it, too? Interference from the city has to be blocking her Knowing.

I did not answer because I did not want to validate her thought process by telling her that I was alone. My parents and Aunt Sara had gone to be with Lyndee for a few days. Aunt Lyndee was having some health issues which they were helping sort out. I said, "I will fix a special supper tonight so don't be late."
I went into the house and looked around the kitchen for some ideas for supper. I found enough fresh vegetables to make a nice platter and found myself arranging them in the image of a little human. Doing this brought a smile to

my Spirit. I looked around for fruit to make features. When I finished, I looked at my creation and realized with a laugh that it looked like a combination of human and some other life form I could not name.

Sam got home and went immediately to wash the city off before coming down to get me at the cabin site. As she walked toward me I saw another glow following her. She did not seem to know it was there. I contained my excitement and refrained from shouting out for her to look behind her.

When she reached me I thought that her greeting was a little more tender than usual. We surveyed the day's progress on our home then walked back to the house in comfortable silence.

She went straight for her favorite tea cup, and I poured the tea I had made earlier into the antique pig cup. I saw the little girl in her every time I watched her drink from that cup. We went into the dining room where I had artfully laid out supper. When her eyes caught the sort-of-humanoid arrangement of food on the platter, she laughingly asked, "So you were awake and present earlier?"

I excitedly spilled out an account of the whole vision. When I paused to take a breath, she asked, "So what are we having?"

I stopped in my tracks as I realized that I was not at all sure how to answer. The question caught me completely off guard. Part of me did not understand it and part of me felt silly for not knowing the answer. I meekly said, "A human with a beautiful laugh." She just looked at me for a long time trying to see what I had seen. Our eyes met, and I knew that she was seeing my vision as her eyes softened and her mouth relaxed.

Her mind separated from my vision as her own took its place. I watch as the beautiful glow that was following her earlier merged with her inner peace. As the colors of her Spirit took in the glow her essence grew brighter and more colorful. Her life force multiplied and became so bright it almost hurt my eyes. She came over and gently took me into the brilliance of the conception of another life.

She looked at me with so much tenderness I thought my heart would explode and said, "We are going to have a baby."

Lucas smiled as he observed the scene with complete peace. Jack had come full circle and was now a man. The time had come for him to lead the family into the future.

I can rest now and view my options without worrying about his future. My agreement is fulfilled.

Coming in
2012

7 Lives Remembered

GY Brown
PH Jones

Chapter 1

The choices were endless at this point. Having lived many lives and learned many things, the choice to go back and experience a life for my own understanding was not an issue. The choice I was making this time was to go back and help the humans get through the last of the barriers to the oneness. I wanted to experience the mass awakening among them. I was entertaining this idea because not only could I take the memories with me, but I would also be allowed to skip infancy this time which was a big deal because none of us liked having no control over our bodies. Those who remembered dreaded infancy.

My objective was clear. I was looking for someone in need of an immediate break, someone on the brink of departing and starting over but hesitating momentarily to consider the consequences of such a premature exit. The place at which that person would start over would be even worse, but if they were replaced instead, they would not have to start over and risk possibly harming an innocent.

I had been in this very position myself once. In a very dark place with no hope of peace, I could not discover the point at which I had agreed to the things that were happening around me. Having stepped off into the agreement of another, I found myself unable to get back to my own. It was during a time of war, and the raping and killing was simply more than I could bear. My mind just left me, and I could not see past the present. My actions had at that point become those of another, and I could no longer remember even the smallest reason for being in that life. I ended it by jumping from a cliff one summer afternoon and flew on the wings of Creation back home to rest while another bravely stepped in to fulfill the agreement which had held me captive. This spirit handled it all much better than I had and went on to help many others. I was grateful to him.

So this time I had a specific situation in mind. The person had to have already gone through enough hurt to know what not to do, as I had. She had to have been trapped in a situation that was not a part of her agreement, with no hope of escaping with honor. She also had to have learned all the things that she was supposed to learn. We were not expected to continually repeat the same events if we had already completed the cycle.

As I viewed my possibilities, I could see so many leaving by their own hand. How could I possibly have made this choice? They were all so young! The pain of being different had altered their minds and Spirits, and they were granting Fear the power to make them consider breaking their life agreements. I communicated with those around me that we simply must help.

How can we possibly stay in this peaceful existence when we see such distress on other levels, knowing we can make it better? How can we stay here knowing that we are needed there? The universal love that is our life force will not permit us to just sit idly by and watch!

One girl in particular drew my attention. She was only 14 Earth years. Human expectations and abuse had gotten to her, and the pressures of the physical were beginning to stifle her Knowing. She was reaching for a prescription bottle.

No! Don't do that! Wait, and I will see if I can relieve you of your agreement and finish it for you!

I turned to the others even as she was emptying the pills into her hand, all the while willing her not to do it. When I turned back after finalizing my agreement, she had already swallowed the contents of the bottle. I froze in horror.

I don't know if we can do this now! She may have already cut the agreement cord that binds her Spirit to the Knowing!

I watched with great regret as she lay down and willed herself to sleep forever, then turned to my Knowing in disbelief. Thought-words transmitted a question to me: **"Do you still want to relieve this one and continue her mission?"**

Made in the USA
Middletown, DE
25 September 2016